MW01069665

"Don't Eat My Pie, Squirt."

DONALD R. RICHARDSON

Don't Eat My Pie, Squirt

Copyright © 2013 by Donald Richardson

All rights reserved.

Printed by Litho Printers & Bindery, Cassville, MO

Cover and interior book design and by Heidi Lowe

First Printed Edition

ISBN 978-1-4675-7888-2

DEDICATED TO THE MEMORY OF
MISSOURI STATE HIGHWAY PATROL TROOPER
VICTOR ORVILLE DOSING

TABLE OF CONTENTS

ACKNOWLEDGMENTS

THIS BOOK WOULD NOT have been possible without the assistance and input from many people. The vast majority of those who helped in some way were from within the family of the Missouri State Highway Patrol. All of those who provided information and input were very eager to help and they all were equally as eager to learn more about this early part of Patrol history. The desire of so many people to become more knowledgeable helped provide the incentive for the writing of this book. It would not be possible for me to recall the names of all of the people who assisted in some way. But for all of you, your support was overwhelming.

I especially want to recognize three individuals. The first is my wife, whose patience and tolerance must have been stretched very thin. For many months nine years ago, and again the past year and one half, she has been a part of my intermittent work on this book. A large table in the basement was covered with my materials, computer, and printer. All of that had to be boxed and moved out of the way many times for family gatherings, and then I would spread it onto the table again. Not a single time did she mention anything about matches or a dumpster. Thank you, Linda.

My cousin, Marie Divita, volunteered to edit and offer suggestions on the book. I doubt that she would make that offer again. She is ultimately qualified as she is "Dr." Marie Divita, a retired college professor. But I don't think she realized how much help her first-time book writer cousin would need. She devoted many hours reading, marking errors, noting suggestions, and talking with me. I am certain many of those hours she was bewildered by what she was reading. I asked her many times to "give it her best shot" and not be concerned about any possibility of offending me. Her efforts were quite obvious when I received the edited manuscript from her. She made notes and corrections in pencil. Had she written in red ink, some portions of the pages would have displayed more red than black and grey. Cousin Marie, your assistance is sincerely appreciated.

Cheryl Cobb is a Public Information Specialist III in the Public Information and Education Division of the Missouri State Highway Patrol. Cheryl loves Patrol history and is very knowledgeable. She was eager to assist in any way she could, and provided a large volume of information and pictures nine years ago when the Dosing Memorial was being planned, and again several times the past one and one-half years. Her assistance was invaluable.

The Dosing and Graham families contributed photographs, stories, suggestions, and support in the planning of the Dosing Memorial and this book. It was a pleasure to become acquainted with them and learn more about the lives of two of the troopers who worked in the early days of the Missouri State Highway Patrol.

Newspapers:

Springfield Daily News, Springfield, Missouri

Springfield Leader and Press, Springfield, Missouri

Arkansas Democrat, Little Rock, Arkansas

Lathrop Optimist, Lathrop, Missouri

Festus Tri-City Independent, Festus, Missouri

The Washington Missourian, Washington, Missouri

The Pulaski County Democrat, Waynesville, Missouri

The Eveleth News, Eveleth, Minnesota

The Cassville Democrat, Cassville, Missouri

Individuals

Sergeant H. P. Bruner, Missouri State Highway Patrol, retired

Lieutenant E. B. Burnam, Missouri State Highway Patrol, retired

Ms. Dee Snider, Springfield, Missouri

Mr. Robert Newman, Greene County Archives and Record Center, Springfield, Missouri

Ms. Shannon Mawhiney, Digitization Specialist, Special Collections and Archives, Duane G. Meyer Library, Missouri State University, Springfield

Ms. Pat Worsham, Rogersville, Missouri

Employees of the Missouri Department of Transportation, Southwest District

Mr. Tom Hollis, Springfield, Missouri

Mr. Gary Miller, Springfield, Missouri

Ms. Saundra Stroud, Springfield, Missouri

Sergeant T. R. Selvey, Missouri State Highway Patrol, retired

Ms. Lena VanHouden, Springfield, Missouri

Mr. Jack McDowell, Springfield, Missouri

Mr. Charles McMillian, Springfield, Missouri

Sergeant M. B. Robertson, Missouri Hightway Patrol, retired

Springfield Daily News

VOL. 51—NO. 342   SPRINGFIELD, MISSOURI, MONDAY MORNING, DECEMBER 8, 1941.   PRICE 3 CENTS

JAPS DECLARE WAR!
HAWAII BOMBARDED!

Highway Patrolman Victor O. Desing (above), was instantly killed and another patrolman, Sam Graham, was badly wounded in a gun battle shortly after noon yesterday at the Coffee Pot, roadside tavern five miles south of Springfield on highway 65, that ended the brief crime career of Milan J. Nedinovich, suspected of two slayings. Tipped that a car stolen after a slaying at Little Rock, Ark., was at the tavern, the two patrolmen went there to investigate. Nedinovich, recently discharged from the army, opened fire as the patrolmen started to open the door to the room where he was with Margie Smith, 19-year-old waitress. Nedinovich, Desing, Graham was then shot. Soon after the ex-soldier died—apparently from his own gun. Full details of the tragedy are reported on PAGE TEN.

BODY OF DUNLAP FOUND AS SEARCH NEARLY GIVEN UP

Veteran River Guide Rube Meadows Leads Party Making Discovery; Sight of Boot Leads to Find

RIVER LEVEL LOWERED BY SHUTDOWN AT DAM

Recovery Made Just Two Weeks After Greene County Surveyor Drowned In Fishing Trip Accident

BODY of Charles H. Dunlap, Greene county surveyor, drowned two weeks ago in the White river near Elbow shoals, was recovered late yesterday afternoon—just as the final search for it was about to be abandoned.

A party of thirteen headed by Rube Meadows, veteran Ozark guide, discovered the body in a 'big slues' to the west side of the river just above the 'Blue hole' shortly before 5 p. m.

Lee Meadows and Floyd Moore, two members of the party, were in the boat that saw the body. They called the other guides—Joe and Rube Meadows, Jr., and Rube Jr.—and the five soon had it out of the water.

BOOT IS SEEN FIRST

Moore saw a boot first, he said. It was later facing that Dunlap, in a supreme effort to save his life, had gotten off one of his hip boots he was wearing. But it was still strapped to his belt. The other boot was still on, as was the heavy coat that he had been wearing.

The body had lodged downstream alongside of a large water-soaked log, and protected by it in such a manner that open books could not reach it. The deep, long halls where it was found, had been dragged many times before. Meadows said, he himself, Moore, and the others guides there too.

The finding of the body ended one of the most intensive searches that has been made for a number of years. The surveyor drowned the night of November 23 when a boat in which he and Joe W. Moore, 200 North Broadway, were going up the river capsized.

HADN'T A CHANCE

Moore, with difficulty, made his way to shore. But Dunlap, who couldn't swim, hadn't a chance in the turbulent water.

The river was rather high at the time, and Moore. First attempts to recover the body failed when the river went down.

Japanese People Promised Victory By Their Premier

LOS ANGELES, Dec. 7—Premier Hideki Tojo told the Japanese people in a broadcast from Tokyo tonight 'I hereby promise you that Japan will win final victory.'

He said Japan was declaring war on the United States for 'self preservation and self existence.'

The broadcast was picked up by the NBC listening post. Tojo appealed to all Japanese in sympathize in the struggle and declared that in 1000 years of military Japan never had lost a war.

BULLETIN

NEW YORK, Monday, Dec 8.—(AP)—NBC reported from Manila early today that it had recorded a report by of a Japanese General Hugh L. Sand and been voiced about 1000 miles from Manila.

First Target Of Japs: Pearl Harbor

PEARL HARBOR—This was the first target of Japanese bombers and was heavily damaged in today's attack.—AP

LEWIS IS WINNER OF CLOSED SHOP

Arbitration Board Rules 2-1 Against Steel In Coal Mine Dispute

NEW YORK, Dec. 7—The United Mine Workers of America (CIO) tonight won a 2-to-1 arbitration board decision awarding a union shop in captive mines owned by the country's major steel producers.

The decision was announced by Dr. John R. Steelman, chairman on the award who was granted it was issued at absence as chairman of the U S. conciliation service to head the arbitration.

Agreed to Abide.

John L. Lewis, president of the mine, agreed with Steelman in the majority opinion. Benjamin F. Fairless, president of the United States Steel corporation, dissented.

The eight steel companies, facing previously agreed to abide by the decision of the board appointed by President Roosevelt after the recent captive mine strike, will be compelled as a result of the board's award to sign the Appalachian wage agreement which it in effect between the union and all but a negligible portion of the country's coal producers.

Only One Issue.

The steel companies already had separate organizations with the union, except they placed lump other wage scales and conditions of the Appalachian agreement in the captive mines in the numerous far the union-mine producers under private, lately Union.

BULLETINS!

WASHINGTON, Monday, Dec. 8.—(UP)— President Roosevelt will address a joint session of congress at 12:30 p. m. today and may ask recognition that a state of war exists between the United States and Japan, and possibly with Germany and Italy.

By The Associated Press
OTTAWA, Dec. 7—(AP)—Canada declared war on Japan tonight.

BATAVIA, Netherlands East Indies, Monday, Dec. 8—(AP)—The Netherlands East Indies declared war on Japan today and immediately proclaimed a state of 'danger of air attack.' The declaration called upon people of these islands for an all-out war against the Japanese empire. The Aneta agency said all Japanese living in the Netherlands East Indies had been interned.

NEW YORK, Dec. 7—(AP)—The air force of the United States in the Far East has taken to the air, an NBC observer reported by radio direct from Manila today.

NEW YORK, Dec. 7—(AP)—An axis-controlled radio station at Shanghai broadcast a Japanese report tonight saying 'a large number of Thai military forces have commenced moving towards the southern border of Burma.' Burma is British.

WASHINGTON, Dec. 7—(AP)—President Roosevelt has authorized the arrest of Japanese nationals regarded as 'dangerous to the peace and security of the United States,' Attorney General Biddle announced tonight. The Justice department estimated that fewer than 1000 Japanese aliens would be affected.

Heavy Casualty List Is Reported At Pearl Harbor

By The Associated Press

Japan assaulted every main United States and British possession in the central and western Pacific and invaded Thailand today in a hasty but evidently shrewdly-planned prosecution of a war she began Sunday without warning.

Her formal declaration of war against both the United States and Britain came two hours and 55 minutes after Japanese planes spread death and terrific destruction in Honolulu and Pearl Harbor at 7:35 a. m., Hawaiian time (12:05 p. m. CST) Sunday.

The claimed successes for this fell swoop included sinking of the U. S. battleship West Virginia and setting afire of the battleship Oklahoma.

From that moment, each tense tick of the clock brought new and flaming accounts of Japanese aggression in her secretly launched war of conquest or death for the land of the rising sun.

As compiled from official and unofficial accounts from all affected countries, the record ran like this:

Honolulu bombed a second time;

Lumber-laden U. S. army transport torpedoed 1300 miles west of San Francisco and another transport in distress;

Shanghai's International Settlement seized; U. S. gunboat Wake captured there and British gunboat Peterel destroyed;

Capture of the U. S. island of Wake;

Bombing of the U. S. island of Guam;

Bombing of many points throughout the Philippine islands;

Invasion of northern Malaya and bombing of Singapore;

Invasion of Thailand (Siam) and bombing of Bangkok.

The first U. S. official casualty report listed 104 dead and more than 300 injured in the army at Hickam Field, alone, near Honolulu. An NBC observer in Honolulu reported the death toll at Hickam was 300.

There was heavy damage in Honolulu residential districts, and the death list among civilians was large but uncounted.

The German radio reported that a sea battle between the Japanese navy on one side and the British and U. S. on the other was in progress in the western Pacific, with a third U. S. warship hit in addition to the West Virginia and Oklahoma.

The British command at Singapore announced the Japanese invasion and said empire forces were engaging the foe.

There was little news of U. S. defensive actions, except the report that a number of the attacking planes at Honolulu had been shot down in dog-fights over the city; an unconfirmed report that a Japanese aircraft carrier had been sunk off Hawaii and

Continued on Page Five

This is the picture of Private Milan J. Nedinovich who shot and killed one highway patrolman and seriously wounded another shortly afternoon yesterday, which was found in the room of Margie Smith, the 19-year-old girl friend, who was questioned concerning the soldier, who was fatally shot soon after he shot the officers.

Sam Graham (above), highway patrol trooper, was in St. John's hospital in a serious, if not critical condition but is light as the result of being shot by an ex-soldier, who he find Graham's partner, trooper Victor O. Desing.

WEST THICKET, Massa.—
bachen A. Lindbergh, visiting at 'un forms farm in the arthka's Vineyard Island village, closed tonight to see newspapermen or accept any messages.

Weather

Nye Says British Planned In This Way

By The United Press
PITTSBURGH, Dec. 7—Senator Gerald P. Nye, republican, N. D., said here tonight that the Japanese attack on the United States was 'just what Britain planned for years.'

Allan speaking to an American audience with his isolationist, mothe and reporters.

'Britain has been getting into ready since 1939.'

The 29,000-ton U. S. battleship Oklahoma (above) was reported ablaze in Pearl Harbor today, following a direct hit by a Japanese bombing plane. It was built in 1916 and took part in the World war. A late dispatch from the Japanese news agency, Domei, claimed the Oklahoma had been sunk.

PREFACE

DECEMBER 7, 1941 is a date that is forever etched in the minds of most Americans. The attack on Pearl Harbor was an unprovoked attack that shocked, angered, and saddened everyone in the country. But for the citizens of Missouri, the Missouri State Highway Patrol, and the residents of the Springfield area, a second tragedy added to their grief. About fifteen to twenty minutes after the attack began on Pearl Harbor, one Missouri trooper was killed and another critically wounded while attempting to question a murder suspect. The December 8, 1941 edition of the *Springfield Daily News* had coverage of the Pearl Harbor attack on the front page, as well as articles about the shooting of the troopers. The last page of the paper was devoted exclusively to pictures and articles of the shooting.

While I was writing this book, several people suggested that I write a few words about myself and why I wrote this book. They believed that a reader could better understand the book if they had some knowledge of the author's background and his motive for writing the book. I was, at first, quite hesitant to write anything about myself. I was not a trooper who received a gunshot wound at the Coffee Pot Tavern in 1941, nor was I a member of the Missouri State Highway Patrol in 1941. I was not a family member of one of the troopers who was shot, and I did not experience the pain and hardship suffered by those family members. However, I finally decided to add a few details about myself with the

PAGE TEN · Springfield Daily News · MONDAY MORNING, DECEMBER 8, 1941.

EX-SOLDIER KILLS PATROLMAN 'VIC' DOSING

Companion Shot; Killer Also Slain

Soldier Traveled Both By Auto, Motorcycle:

Girl Describes Her Many Dates With Slayer of State Trooper

A blaze of gunfire at the Coffee Pot, night spot about five miles south of Springfield on highway 65 shortly after afternoon yesterday left Highway Patrolman Victor O. Dosing lying dead. Patrolman Sam Graham gravely wounded—and ended with a bullet the brief criminal career of Milan J. Nedimovich, suspected of two slayings and several auto thefts in Missouri and Arkansas.

At first it was thought that Justice A. F. Stubbs of Galloway killed Nedimovich, with a gun belonging to the soninlaw of John Hoffman, watchman, Little Rock, Ark., officers believe, he the ex-soldier.

THE story of how Private Milan James Nedimovich, slayer of Highway Patrolman Victor O. Dosing, spent considerable time in and around Springfield, hurling dates with her, is told in the following statement which Margie Fae Smith made to Sheriff Earl Womack and County Attorney Bill Collinson yesterday afternoon.

Up these stairs to the door at the top of them, State Patrolmen Victor Dosing and Sam Graham walked about noon yesterday.—Dosing to his death and Graham to receive serious wounds. The door opens into the room occupied by Margie Smith, on the second floor of the Coffee Pot, on highway 65 south of Galloway. Through it Private Milan J. Nedimovich fired at the two patrolmen.—(Daily News Staff Photo)

Margie Smith, 19-year-old waitress whose home is at Walnut Grove, is shown in her room at the Coffee Pot shortly after a gun battle in which her fiance, Private Milan J. Nedimovich, and State Patrolman Victor O. Dosing were killed and Patrolman Sam S. Graham was wounded. Yesterday afternoon and last night, Sheriff Earl Womack and County Attorney Bill Collinson questioned the Smith girl closely about the dead soldier's movements and later release her to her employers.—(Daily News Staff Photo)

CONSTABLE SAYS ARMY WAS LAX

This is the scene of the shooting yesterday which ended in death for a state patrolman and a soldier AWOL, and serious injuries for another patrolman. The place is the Coffee Pot cafe, on highway 65 just south of Galloway. A crowd began gathering soon after the shooting, as the picture shows.—(Daily News Staff Photo)

LUMBER
Per 100 Board Feet
—Specials—

$3.06
$3.50
$2.50
$1.35

HOEY
Coal & Lbr. Co.
418 W. Chase St.

anticipation that some readers might find that information beneficial as they attempt to interpret my logic in what I have written.

I was born in Eldon, Missouri and attended school there through high school, graduating in 1963. I enrolled at Central Missouri State College in Warrensburg, receiving a Bachelor of Science Degree in Education in 1967. I was a teacher and coach for two years at small schools and then became a member of the Missouri State Highway Patrol in 1969. In 1974 I received a Bachelor of Science Degree in Law Enforcement from Drury College in Springfield. In 1984 I received a Master of Science Degree in Law Enforcement Administration from Central Missouri State College in Warrensburg.

For twenty nine years I "worked the road" as a member of the Patrol. For the last eleven of those years I was a supervisor as a sergeant. I then transferred into Troop D Headquarters where I had various assignments for another six years. Retirement came in 2004 after thirty-five years of service, all in the Springfield area.

The majority of information for this book was accumulated in 2003 and 2004. It began with research for the planning of the memorial to honor of Trooper Vic Dosing, who was killed on December 7, 1941. I became curious about the shootings. Curiosity developed into a fascination with the unusual events surrounding the shootings that day. I began acquiring every bit of information I could locate. I found that many of those bits of information were incomplete and inaccurate. I decided to write a book to document as many of the events related to the Coffee Pot Tavern shooting of Troopers Dosing and Graham as possible.

However, work on the book was postponed for too many years as I struggled with my belief that the story of the Coffee Pot shootings would be incomplete without the information on the other two murders committed by the troopers' assailant. He murdered three men at three different locations within a time period of two weeks. All three men had families and two left grieving widows who were expecting another child. There were too many interesting pieces of the puzzle that tied all three murders together, other than the fact that the same man was responsible for all three. On the other hand, the law enforcement officer part of me could hardly accept the thought of a killer receiving more space in the text of a murder story than a trooper he killed and another he critically wounded. I finally resolved my indecision by talking with a member of the Dosing and Graham families. They encouraged me to include information on the other two murders.

Work then began on the book without that nagging hesitancy that had ended the progress for years. The reader will have to determine if the account of the shooting of the two troopers would have been complete without the inclusion of information from the other two murders. Did that addition diminish the accomplishment of the goal of writing this book: To honor the ultimate sacrifice of Trooper Vic Dosing?

There are portions of the book that are subjective in nature and reflect my personal philosophy. That philosophy was developed from my career, and life in general, based on experiences, training, and education. The reader may decide that some of what I have written seems to be based on the ideals and opinions of an "Old Timer." The reason I included anything about myself was to allow the reader to become somewhat familiar with my perspective. If the reader decides the book must have been written by an "Old Timer," I will not be offended. Rather, I will be very pleased. I am quite proud of my long career with the Missouri State Highway Patrol and my nine years of retirement. It would be an honor to be considered an "Old Timer".

Missouri State Highway Patrol Trooper Victor Orville Dosing was shot to death December 7, 1941. Trooper Samuel Stanley Graham was also shot and nearly perished from his wound. The original intent of my research was to document, in as much detail as possible, the events surrounding the shootings. I also added information about the lives of Vic Dosing and Sam Graham, the Dosing funeral and Dosing Memorial, questions that developed during the book research, and an appendix containing law enforcement documents. Information will be presented in chronological order.

Research from law enforcement records for this project was limited to three documents: Missouri State Highway Patrol Sergeant Oliver Viets' report, the written statement of Margie Smith, and the coroner's inquest transcript. Most of the information that had been contained in the files of the Missouri State Highway Patrol could no longer be located. None of the police agencies involved in the three murders have reports dating to 1941. Much of my information for this history has, by necessity, been obtained from newspaper articles. Further complicating research was the fact that the Springfield Newspaper files were destroyed by a fire in 1949 and there were few original photographs available. The newspapers were available on microfilm at the library, but the film was of very mediocre quality.

The three law enforcement documents are included in the appendix of this book. They were reproduced verbatim so that they could be condensed and more legible.

The Dosing murder was a complicated event in which at least a total of nine rounds were fired from five weapons. Some of the preliminary information typed just over two hours after the shooting, some newspaper accounts, and even portions of the testimony at the coroner's inquest the following day, was inaccurate because the investigation had not been completed. The report by Patrol Sergeant O. L. Viets is more accurate because it was completed after the investigation and ballistics analysis had been finished.

Margie Smith was a waitress at the Coffee Pot Tavern and fiancée of U. S. Army Private Milan James Nedimovich. She provided a detailed statement to Sheriff Ruel Wommack and Greene County Prosecuting Attorney William Collison a few hours after the Dosing and Graham shootings. It was reprinted in the newspaper, and if completely truthful and accurate, provides a valuable timeline of the relationship of Margie Smith and Milan James Nedimovich to the murders. It contains many comments Nedimovich made to Margie which were obviously untruthful.

There were at least two articles written for detective magazines about the Dosing murder. Both articles were highly glamorized and contained many errors. One was written more than one year later, and the other fourteen years later. I will not cite those articles, or use any information contained in them, because I don't want to publicize material, which in my opinion, is inaccurate and fictionalized. Any reader who might have access to those articles should be cautioned to expect errors and advised to also read the coroner's inquest testimony and Sergeant O. L. Viet's report for the most accurate accounts of the shootings.

The Missouri Legislature had created the Missouri State Highway Patrol in 1931. Vic Dosing and Oliver L. Viets were members of the first recruit class and were the two original members stationed in Springfield. In November, 1938, Vic and his young family moved to their home at 954 East Kingsbury in Springfield. On December 7, 1941 the family of 34-year-old Victor Dosing included his wife Rosalie, and daughters Jo Ann, aged 8, and Janet, aged 2 ½. Rosalie was pregnant and their third child was expected in February.

On that Sunday morning Rosalie had prepared the family dinner early because Vic was scheduled to report for duty at noon. She had baked a chocolate pie, Vic's favorite. As the family was eating dinner the phone rang. That call required Vic to leave for work. As Vic told Jo Ann goodbye at the front door he said, "**Don't eat my pie, Squirt**," Vic's nickname for his oldest daughter. That was the last time the family would see Vic.

"Don't Eat My Pie, Squirt."

CHAPTER ONE

THE MURDERS

IN 1941, GALLOWAY, MISSOURI was a small town located in Clay Township of Greene County. At that time, Galloway was more than three miles south of Springfield. It is now within the Springfield city limits at the southeast corner. Highway 65 ran through the town and the railroad served the community with a depot. The railroad line ran from Springfield to Ozark and Chadwick. Sequiota Spring was at the north edge of the town beside the highway and railroad tracks, and was a popular family destination. People in Springfield would often ride the train to Galloway and enjoy a picnic at Sequiota Spring.

About one and one-half miles south of Galloway the highway crossed the James River. Just southeast of the bridge the highway split and Highway 65 turned south toward Ozark and Highway 60 curved east up the hill toward Rogersville.

The Coffee Pot Tavern was located on Highway 65 southeast of Springfield. It was four-tenths of a mile south of the town of Galloway on the west side of the highway. It was on a tract of land measuring 168 feet east and west, and 588 feet north and south. It sat between the highway and a small stream which was on the east side of the railroad tracks.

The land was owned by Lula Galloway, who leased it to Sam W. Baker. On September 4, 1941, the land and buildings were sub-leased by Sam Baker to U. R. and Rachel Coble for thirty-five dollars per month.

The Coffee Pot Tavern was a small white building actually built in the shape of a coffee pot. It was round and approximately twenty-five feet in diameter at the base. The sides tapered in with a "spout" on the front and a "handle" on the rear. The kitchen extended from the rear of the building. The foot of the stairway to the upstairs room was near the kitchen exterior door. The Coffee Pot sat no more than forty feet from the edge of the highway in a grove of walnut trees. Behind the building was a dance pavilion with a white picket fence around it.

The Coffee Pot Tavern as it appeared a few years
before the December 7, 1941 shooting.

Margie Fae Smith was nineteen years old and the youngest of eight children. She attended high school in Walnut Grove, Missouri. On April 10, 1941 she began working as a waitress at the Coffee Pot Tavern, living in the room above the tavern.

Near the end of September or the first part of October, 1941, Margie Smith met a soldier in uniform at Amy's Grill on South Jefferson in Springfield. He said his name was Jimmy Donnahue and that he was stationed at Ft. Leonard Wood. They began dating and they were together nearly every evening during the first week of October. He was driving a 1937 Buick. Then, she did not see him for about one month.

John Love was a deputy constable for the Galloway area attached to the court of Justice of the Peace J. A. Stubbs. They were good friends and were often together. On October 9, they checked a Buick that appeared suspicious. They found a soldier, identified as twenty year-old Milan James Nedimovich, asleep in the rear seat. Constable Love later said the soldier admitted stealing the car from a used car lot in St. Louis, Missouri. It was fortunate that Nedimovich was taken into custody peaceably as neither Love nor Stubbs was armed.

Constable Love checked with Troop D Headquarters of the Missouri State Highway Patrol in Springfield and learned that troopers had been watching for the soldier after being notified by Ft. Leonard Wood officials that he was AWOL. Constable Love said Nedimovich was turned over to the Highway Patrol.

Retired Patrol Lieutenant E. B. Bur-

Margie Smith is shown in her room above the Coffee Pot following the shootings. (Springfield Daily News)

This picture of Milan James Nedimovich was taken some time before the shootings. (Springfield Daily News)

nam recalled the day Troopers Dosing and Graham arrived at Troop D Headquarters with Milan James Neidmovich, who was in uniform. Lieutenant Burnam and several other troopers had been on the firing range. He said Nedimovich did not cause any problems while they were at headquarters.

Nedimovich was taken to the Greene County Jail by Trooper Vic Dosing. It is unknown if Trooper Graham accompanied them to the jail. The jail booking sheet indicated Nedimovich was 6'1" in height, weighed 170 pounds, and had brown hair, blue eyes, and a dark complexion. He was from Eveluth, Minnesota and was drafted into the U.S. Army on July 18, 1941. He was arrested for "Inv" (Investigation). Other jail records indicated he was arrested on "65 Highway So" and was released at 1:50 PM on October 10 to Sgt. Connor from Ft. Leonard Wood.

The troopers, Constable Love and Justice Stubbs probably had a very reasonable belief that Nedimovich would be in the custody of the Army for some time, and when released, would be charged with the theft of the Buick in St. Louis. It would have been logical to think he would be off the streets for quite some time.

Margie Smith's later statements indicate she did not see Donnahue for a period of about four weeks after the first part of October. She said she then saw him on a Saturday when he apparently revealed to her his real name was Milan James Nedimovich. He told her he had used the fictitious name because he had told a former girlfriend his real name and he was expecting problems from her. Margie Smith continued to call him "Jimmy."

Nedimovich had been released from the Greene County Jail to Ft. Leonard Wood on October 10. If the statement by Margie Smith was completely accurate, she probably saw him on October 7 or 8, the day before his arrest. She saw him next on a Saturday about four weeks later, probably November 1, and possibly for a time on Sunday, November 2.

He had obviously told her he was being transferred to Camp Robinson at Little Rock, Arkansas. On November 6, she wrote a letter addressed to him at Camp Robinson. In the letter she said, "Darling, I wish I could see you. I've something to tell you. I hope you will deny it, but I don't think you will. It's something you don't think I know. Honey, it don't make any difference to me. I heard it Sun. night right after you left, so I went to Galloway to try and find you but you were gone. Darling, you weren't at Scott Field at all were you. Come darling tell me the truth. Jimmy, remember you told me the only lie you had told me was about your name, honey, I hope you're right." They had talked about getting married and in that same letter she had also written, "God, darling, army or no army you're mine aren't you, Honey, if you wanted me down there or do you – as bad as I want you up here, hell and high water couldn't hold me. Honey, aren't you ever going to send me an engagement ring or are you? Maybe you're not that serious. I don't know, I've worn out my brain trying to figure you out. Darling, I like yellow gold."

Margie Smith saw Nedimovich the middle of November and then again late the evening of Sunday, November 23 or early morning of November 24. He was riding a motorcycle on this visit to Galloway. She was with him that afternoon from 1:00 PM until about 5:30 PM. She was supposed to have a date with him that evening and again on the 25th at 10:00 AM. He did not show up either time. That afternoon she went to a movie in Springfield and was at the Union Bus Station to ride the bus back to Galloway when Nedimovich came in with their friend, Velma Jones. All three rode the motorcycle back to the Coffee Pot where she changed clothes. They returned to Springfield where they went to Gilmore's, the Flying A Terminal, and back to Gilmore's. Later in the evening they took Velma Jones to her home on North Prospect and then drove to the Coffee Pot, arriving just after midnight. Nedimovich stayed at the Coffee Pot until about 1:30 PM, November 26 when he left southbound on Highway 65, saying he needed to be at roll call the next morning in Little Rock.

Nedimovich walked into the Coffee Pot at about 9:30 PM, Saturday, November 29. He informed Margie that he had ridden the bus from Little Rock. They went to a few taverns with another couple in their car. Sometime during the evening, Nedimovich gave Margie an engagement ring, and later, a wedding ring in a box with a Sass Jewelry label on it. They let Nedimovich out at the front door of the Met Hotel on College Street. He mentioned getting a room for the night and walked into the lobby. Those rings were purchased on November 28 and apparently paid for with the estimated thirty-five dollars stolen from his first murder victim.

§§§§§§§§§§§§§§

Ernest H. Newman was a native of Cassville, Missouri. The twenty-eight year-old had been married in 1934 to Lyndell Plumlee. They had moved to St. Louis and later to Washington, Missouri, where Ernest operated a service station. Their son, Harry Dee, was six years of age and Lyndell Newman was expecting a second child near the end of November, 1941.

Between 9:00 PM and 10:00 PM on Wednesday, November 26, Ernest Newman received a telegram from Cassville which indicated his mother was very ill. He began driving westbound to Cassville in a 1932 Ford shortly after receiving the telegram.

At about 4:00 AM on November 27 Newman stopped at the Oak Grove Lodge which was located about three miles east of Strafford on Highway 66. He awakened Virgil Sechler, the station operator, and asked if he could buy some gas, explaining that he was trying to get to Cassville to see his ill mother. Sechler unlocked the pump and let Newman pump the gas himself. Newman paid with a five dollar bill he removed from a roll of money. It was later determined Newman had approximately thirty-five dollars with him. Newman was accompanied by a soldier in uniform.

When Earnest Newman failed to arrive at his parent's home in Cassville on Thursday, his family began to worry. When he did not make an appearance on Friday, they became very concerned and notified law enforcement agencies. They also began their own search.

For two or three days there was a very intensive search for Earnest Newman. Family members, friends, the Missouri State Highway Patrol, sheriff's deputies, and soldiers from Fort Leonard Wood participated in canvassing businesses along the highway from Washington, Missouri to Cassville, Missouri.

The search and publicity did result in the development of the information provided by Virgil Sechler of Oak Grove Lodge. At that point investigators had a suspect description of a soldier. Several AWOL soldiers were arrested and interrogated. One AWOL soldier and his cousin were arrested in a stolen car and questioned at Jefferson City. They admitted stealing four cars but denied knowledge of Newman's death. Virgil Sechler could not identify either as the soldier who had been with Newman at the Oak Grove Lodge. Until I realized Nedimovich had been transferred to Camp Robinson, I wondered why he had not been on a list of AWOL Fort Leonard Wood soldiers questioned following Newman's disappearance.

On Sunday afternoon, November 30, a farmer found Ernest Newman's car abandoned in a wooded area off a county road about eight miles west of Waynesville. A few items of clothing were missing from the car. The search continued for Ernest Newman. Newspaper reports indicated that a study of the service records on Newman's car suggested it had been driven about fifty miles farther than the total distance from Washington to the Oak Grove Lodge, and then to the place where it was abandoned.

At about 1:30 PM, Sunday, November 30, Nedimovich stopped by the Coffee Pot and told Margie he had to get back to Little Rock. He got into the passenger seat of a car waiting for him. He was dressed in a uniform.

Around 5:00 PM the next day Margie found him sitting in the Coffee Pot. He said he had been waiting about an hour. He told her he had worked about a half hour that morning in Little Rock until his sergeant gave him release papers from the army, and then given him a ride to Springfield. He left the Coffee Pot about 11:00 PM to hitch-hike to Little Rock saying he would return about Friday, December 5.

Margie's statement indicated Mr. and Mrs. Coble saw Nedimovich in the Coffee Pot about 2:30 or 3:00 PM on Tuesday, December 2.

On Thursday, December 4, Ernest Newman's body was found by a boy walking through the woods to a neighbor's house, some distance from where his car had been located. He had been shot two times with a .38 caliber revolver. One bullet entered his chest and the other the back of his head. The *Cassville Republican* newspaper reported on December 11 that Newman's body was found "about one-half mile off a country road, about two miles from Highway 66." Newman was buried at his home town of Cassville on December 7. His wife was unable to make the trip from Washington to Cassville because she had given birth to a son December 6.

§§§§§§§§§§§§§

John Hoffman was sixty-five years of age and was employed as a night watchman at Owen Motor Company near Second and Spring Streets in Little Rock, Arkansas. On Friday evening, December 5, salesman Walter Aldridge left the business at 7:30 PM after saying goodnight to John Hoffman.

At 7:00 AM the next morning Aldridge found Hoffman beaten to death in the small office and a metallic colored 1939 Packard coupe stolen. The keys to all of the vehicles had been removed from Hoffman's pocket. Police officers first thought the murder weapon was similar to a tire iron. The coroner later suggested the time of death was approximately midnight and that a hammer might have been used in the murder.

Police detectives were informed the Packard had only a small amount of fuel in its tank. Officers began contacting the service stations in an attempt to locate where the killer might have obtained fuel for the Packard. Attendants at a station at 11th and Main in Little Rock informed the officers that a soldier in uniform had stopped about 10:00 PM. He was driving a Packard and said he had been in a fight and his money was stolen. There was blood on his uniform. The attendants agreed to let the soldier leave the spare tire and wheel as security for sixteen gallons of gas and two quarts of oil. The soldier agreed to return to pay for the gas and retrieve the tire and wheel. He signed the receipt with a fictitious name. In addition, the attendants recorded the vehicle license number on the Packard, Arkansas 41-212. That license had been on the Packard when it was stolen.

Little Rock police checked with US Army officials at Camp Robinson in Little Rock for AWOL soldiers who might match the description given them by the service station attendants. It was determined that the best suspect was Claudie D. Davis, age 25, and 5' 11" in height and weighing 150 pounds. He had previously been stationed at Ft. Leonard Wood in Missouri. His description, along with information on the stolen Packard and license plate number, was sent to the Missouri State Highway Patrol Troop D Headquarters by teletype on December 6. The Patrol shared that information with the Greene County Sheriff's Department and the Springfield Police Department. The Springfield newspaper published an article about the Hoffman murder and stolen vehicle information in the Sunday morning edition.

§§§§§§§§§§§§§§

Jimmie Nedimovich left a suitcase at a restaurant at 236 West Commercial in Springfield at 8:30 AM on Saturday, December 6. Restaurant operator Elda Cunningham later gave the suitcase to the sheriff's office. Sheriff's officials found clothing, personal items, and several letters written by Margie Smith to Nedimovich. The December 8 edition of the *Springfield Leader and Press* printed a picture of Greene County Deputy Sheriff Arthur Mace as he examined the contents of that suitcase. Mace is holding "a hypodermic syringe commonly used by 'dope' addicts." However, "the needle was missing from the syringe, and no narcotics were found in the bag. Mace said the instrument could have been used for cold serum."

Margie next saw Nedimovich on Saturday, December 6, about 10:30 PM. He arrived at the Coffee Pot driving a Packard coupe. They left about 11:45 PM and drove to Springfield, stopping at Gilmore's and the Oasis before returning to the Coffee Pot between 3:00 AM and 3:30 AM. They had planned on getting married the following weekend and were to leave for a honeymoon in Florida.

Springfield police officer John Rollins, early in the morning of December 7, observed a car with Arkansas plates and occupied by a young couple eastbound on St. Louis Street at Kimbrough. It stopped at a service station just west of Dollison briefly and then continued east. It stopped at another service station a few blocks farther east. Officer Rollins did not stop. He thought the driver probably wanted to find a place to air a tire. The vehicle had first interested him because of the large number of stolen cars at that time. He realized later that day that the vehicle had probably been occupied by Jimmie Nedimovich and Margie Smith. He most certainly speculated about what might have happened had he approached the vehicle.

When Margie and Nedimovich returned to the Coffee Pot they went upstairs and found the door locked. They awakened Lela Nix, who unlocked the door and let them in. Lela Nix worked at the Coffee Pot on weekends and shared the room with Margie. Margie asked Lela if Nedimovich could stay there until morning. Lela had replied, "Suit yourself." Nedimovich slept in his clothes on the studio couch.

Murder victim John Hoffman of Little Rock was survived by his wife and eight children. One of his daughters, Eustina, was married to George Standke. On Sunday morning, December 7, George and Eustina Standke were driving from their home in Kansas City to Little Rock for John Hoffman's funeral.

Late in the morning they stopped at Fat Jones' Service Station, which was located about one-fourth of a mile south of the Coffee Pot on the west side of the highway.

Fat Jones had read the Springfield newspaper article that morning about the Little Rock murder of John Hoffman. As he and Standke talked, their conversation became centered on the Standke drive to Little Rock for the Hoffman funeral. Jones then remembered the newspaper article about the murder with the stolen Packard and soldier description. He remembered he had seen a Packard parked behind the Coffee Pot earlier in the morning and thought it was the same that stopped at his station the evening before. The driver had traded a tire and wheel for gas.

Jones was somewhat familiar with Jimmie Nedimovich, who had visited his station several times the previous two months when he was in the area dating Margie Smith. He remembered Constable Love and Justice Stubbs had arrested Nedimovich in the stolen Buick on October 9. He thought the soldier they had arrested was the same man who had stopped at the station the night before. Standke then drove by the Coffee Pot to look at the Packard. He returned to Jones's Station and told Fat Jones he was certain the Packard was his father-in-law's car.

Jones and Standke apparently went to Justice Stubbs' office. Stubbs called Love and asked him if he remembered the name of the soldier the two had arrested two months earlier in the stolen Buick. Love remembered some of the difficult name and details. Stubbs asked Love to come to his office. When he arrived, Jones and Standke were there. Standke asked Love to call the Patrol, which he did. He informed the person with whom he talked at Troop D Headquarters that they thought the killer of John Hoffman in Little Rock was in the neighborhood. That Patrol employee asked them to return to Jones' Service Station.

Jones, Love, and Standke returned to Jones' Station. Stubbs, for a time, took care of other duties. When they arrived at Jones' Station, Jones told Love that he was certain that the Packard parked behind the Coffee Pot was the same one that had been in his station the evening before.

Love then drove to the Coffee Pot. He went in and asked U. R. Coble if the Packard belonged to Nedimovich. Coble replied that it did and, when asked if Nedimovich was upstairs, stated that he was. Love drove to Jones' Station and asked Jones to call the Patrol. Love and Standke then returned to a position just south of the Coffee Pot and parked on the northbound shoulder to wait for troopers. A short time later Justice Stubbs arrived and parked behind Love. He sat in the car with them.

U.R. Coble said that Nedimovich had arrived at the Coffee Pot about 10:30 PM on Saturday night, December 6. He had stayed outside for a while, apparently because the Coffee Pot was busy. When Coble had a break in his business, he stepped out the rear door and saw that the car Nedimovich had arrived in was a Packard coupe.

On Sunday morning Coble was again in the Coffee Pot with his wife Rachel. Lela Nix came down from the upstairs room between 9:00 AM and 9:30 AM. Margie Smith and Nedimovich were both still asleep at that time. Margie went down for breakfast between 10:00 AM and 10:30 AM. Coble was reading the Sunday paper while Margie was eating breakfast. He noticed the article about the Hoffman murder in Little Rock. He became suspicious when he read that a Packard coupe had been stolen from the murder scene. After Margie finished breakfast, she asked Coble if she could have the paper if he was finished reading it. He said that he was not yet finished. He said nothing to Margie about the Little Rock murder and she returned to the upstairs room.

After Margie left the room the Cobles and Lela Nix began discussing the newspaper article. Coble went outside and obtained the license number from the Packard and wrote the information on the newspaper. Lela Nix had returned to the upstairs briefly two or three times during the morning and said Nedinmovich was still asleep the last time she went up. She apparently did not return to the upstairs room after her conversation with the Cobles about the Little Rock murder.

U. R. Coble was deliberating whether or not to drive to a phone to call the Patrol. Lela Nix later testified that five to ten minutes after Margie returned to the upstairs room, Constable Love walked in and inquired about the Packard and Nedimovich. Love left, apparently telling them he would be back later. He drove to Jones' Station and asked Jones to call the Patrol and a few minutes later Coble noticed Love's car parked along the highway just south of the Coffee Pot. Coble later said that it was probably twenty minutes before the troopers arrived.

It is not known exactly when Trooper Vic Dosing's phone rang late Sunday morning as he was eating an early dinner with his family. That call instructed him and Trooper Sam Graham to check information phoned in by Constable Love and Fat Jones from Jones' Service Station a few minutes earlier. That information pertained to the possibility that the Packard stolen from the Hoffman murder scene in Little Rock was at the Coffee Pot, as well as the man who had driven it there. The troopers drove to the scene in one patrol car.

Nedimovich had probably awakened sometime after 10:30 AM. After Margie Smith returned to her room upstairs they talked about their plans to get married a few days later. As they talked Nedimovich walked to a window and looked out after he heard a car drive onto the gravel parking lot. He did not mention the patrol car occupied by the troopers to Margie.

The troopers walked into the front of the Coffee Pot. They asked U. R. Coble where Nedimovich was and were told he was upstairs. They asked how to get to the room upstairs and were instructed to go out the kitchen door in the rear of the building and up the stairs. Constable

Love had driven onto the Coffee Pot parking lot and entered the building just as the troopers were going out the kitchen door. He yelled at them to "wait a minute" but they apparently did not hear him. He hurried through the building and joined the troopers as they went up the narrow stairway.

Justice Stubbs stepped from the car as he saw the officers start up the stairs. He did not have a weapon but Standke gave his Colt thirty-eight caliber revolver to him to use. Stubbs asked if he could depend on it and Standke replied, "You sure can." Stubbs hurried to a location ten or fifteen feet from the stairway.

The troopers drew their weapons as they started up the stairs at approximately 12:10 to 12:15 PM Sunday. Dosing led the way, followed by Graham and then Constable Cole, who retrieved his pistol from his coat pocket. The stairway was narrow and the straightness was interrupted two times as it angled around the circular curvature of the building. The landing at the top would have been very small, if one even existed.

Margie Smith and Nedimovich heard the footsteps on the stairway. Margie did not know who was approaching the room, but Nedimovich obviously did. Nedimovich produced a pistol as Trooper Dosing reached the top of the stairway. Dosing opened the outer door with his left hand and an instant later Nedimovich quickly opened the inner door and fired one shot which struck Dosing between the eyes, killing him instantly. Dosing fell forward, partially into the room. Nedimovich fired a second round at Graham, who was two or three steps lower than Dosing on the stairway. That bullet struck Graham in the chest. Graham fired one round, but that was only after Dosing had fallen into the room. He was directly behind Dosing on the narrow stairs and could not fire because Dosing had been in the line of fire until after he fell. Constable Love fired two rounds from his .32 caliber pistol. None of those shots struck Nedimovich. Graham staggered from his wound and Love helped him down the stairs and into the kitchen.

Love stayed in the kitchen and watched the bottom portion of the stairway through the windows. Graham walked into the main room and asked the Cobles for the phone. U. R. Coble replied that there was no phone there. Graham then walked out the front door, got into the patrol car, and drove four-tenths of a mile to Galloway where he found Gooch's Store. He went inside and called Troop D Headquarters for help. The patrol car was equipped with a radio that could only receive transmissions; it was not capable of two-way transmission.

Nedimovich started down the stairway a short time after Graham and Love made it into the kitchen. The kitchen roof overhang obstructed Love's view of the top half of the stairway. When he saw Nedimovich's legs he fired two times, one time through each of two windows, and then his pistol malfunctioned. Nedimovich retreated back up the stairs.

Justice Stubbs, positioned outside and beside the stairway, said he did not fire as Nedimovich descended the stairs because he knew there were people inside the building. After Nedimovich returned to the upstairs room, he did fire one shot from Standke's revolver as Nedimovich was in the doorway.

Margie Smith was in the center of the room when the first shot was fired. She testified she ran behind a small coat closet and looked out the window. Nedimovich had apparently started down the stairway and quickly returned as she looked out the window. She said when she looked at him again he was standing with his back to the wall next to the door. She said she called out, "Jimmy," and he told her to "Shut up," pointed his pistol at her and pulled the trigger. She heard it snap as it misfired. He threw the gun to the floor as she began screaming and tried to hide behind an ironing board. When she looked up she saw him falling to the floor.

Danny Jones was a high school student and nephew of Fat Jones, owner of Jones' Service Station. He was in Gooch's Store when Graham went in to use the phone. He said Graham had blood on his uniform. Graham used the phone to call for help. He then went back outside where he briefly hesitated before getting back into the patrol car and driving back toward the Coffee Pot. Jones walked to the Coffee Pot and he thought he arrived before any responding officers.

At approximately 12:20 PM Highway Patrol Sergeant Viets received a call at his home from Sheriff Ruel N. Wommack informing him that he had received information on the stolen Packard from Arkansas. He asked Viets to meet him at Sheriff Wommack's office in about a half hour. He would try to learn more about the stolen car.

About ten minutes later, possibly between 12:25 PM and 12:30 PM, Viets received a call from Patrol Captain R. R. Reed informing him he had sent Troopers Dosing and Graham to Galloway to investigate the stolen Packard. Captain Reed had just received a report that both had been shot. Viets immediately drove to the scene, probably arriving between 12:30 PM and 12:35 PM.

Viets would probably normally have been the first responding officer on the scene. But when he arrived he found a most unusual, but very welcome, sight. There were already four troopers present: Sergeant O. L. Wallis, and Troopers E. E. Barkley, C. B. Bidewell, and N. C. Brill.

Those four troopers had attended the funeral the previous afternoon at Lathrop, Missouri for Trooper Fred L. Walker. Trooper Walker had been the second Missouri State Highway Patrolman to have died in the line of duty.

On December 2, Walker had arrested two young men, aged seventeen and twenty, near Bloomsdale in St. Genevieve County following a chase. He searched and handcuffed them, and placed them in the rear seat of his patrol car. He had driven only a half mile when one of them produced a weapon Trooper Walker had not found, and shot him in the right side of the chest, the bullet piercing both lungs. They threw Trooper Walker out the car and drove off. Walker crawled or hobbled to the farmyard where he had made the arrests. That property owner drove Walker to Crystal City to a doctor and he was transferred to Barnes Hospital in St. Louis. He died the next morning at 10:45 A.M.

A very intensive search lasted almost a full day. A few of the first Patrol cars equipped with two-way radios were used during the manhunt. The Patrol had acquired ten FM two-way radios in 1941 for use on a trial basis. The experiment was very successful and the remainder of the patrol cars were equipped with the new radios in 1942.

The four troopers returning home from the Walker funeral had traveled through Dixon before driving to Springfield. It is unknown where they stayed the night of December 6. They stopped at Troop D Headquarters, located at that time on the southwest corner of what is now Seminole and Fremont in Springfield. A portion of that old head-quarters building remains as it was incorporated into the construction of the Ray Kelly Senior Citizens Center. The troopers were assigned in the general area of Willow Springs, at the time located in the Patrol's Troop E.

They had just left Troop D Headquarters and were near the National Cemetery, about a mile east, when they were given a radio call instructing them to go to the shooting scene at the Coffee Pot, about four miles east and south of their location. As they approached the Coffee Pot at about 12:30 PM they found Trooper Graham's patrol car about two hundred and fifty feet north of the building. When Trooper Graham saw them he got out of the car "all bent over and said he had been shot." He added that the shooter was still upstairs.

After Nedimovich fell to the floor dead, Margie began screaming for a period of time she said could have been two or three minutes. Love and Coble agreed with that statement. When no one came up the stairs she went down and either fell or collapsed at the foot of the stairs. She was helped inside by Love and Coble.

Justice Stubbs' account of the time lapse between his shot at Nedi-movich and the emergence of Margie from the room differed. Stubbs testified at the coroner's inquest that "just as he went in she came out. It wasn't but just a flash."

Love had his revolver working properly again just as Margie came down the stairs. He aimed the weapon again through the kitchen window when he heard footsteps on the stairway but then saw that the legs becoming visible were those of Margie. After she entered the kitchen Standke got out of Love's vehicle and walked to Stubbs. Someone inside the Coffee Pot yelled for them to go somewhere to call for more help. Stubbs did run to Jones' Station to call the Patrol and informed the person he talked with that Dosing had been killed and Graham wounded.

After the four responding troopers talked to Graham they went to the Coffee Pot and surrounded the building, one on each side. Sergeant Wallis went to the south side and talked with Margie and at least one of the men. Margie said that both Dosing and Nedimovich were dead, but her statement was met with caution. She offered to go up with the officers, and according to her testimony, she led the way up the stairs with Sergeant Wallis, Trooper Barkley, and others following. Constable Love said the troopers and others climbed to the upstairs room ten to fifteen minutes after the last shot was fired.

Trooper Barkley testified that when the troopers first went up the stairs, they found Dosing lying face down in the room with his feet extending across the door sill. Nedimovich was lying on his left side at a right angle to Dosing, with his head against the wall and his feet near Dosing's head.

Sergeant Viets arrived just after other troopers had gone upstairs. Sheriff Wommack arrived soon after Viets at about 12:40 PM. Viets asked Sheriff Wommack to take possession of the evidence. They all began the difficult task of attempting to determine exactly what had happened. Early information obtained from the scene was reported to Troop D Headquarters and then relayed by telephone to General Headquarters in Jefferson City. The following teletype message was transmitted throughout the state relaying that very early information.

2-30pm   12-7-41

The following information recd by phone from Capt. Reed and Sgt. O. L. Wallis:

Info recd from an unknown party that subject wanted for murder in Little Rock 12-6-41 was at Galloway. A short time later a man who said he was the son-in-law of the Little Rock victim called Troop D and said subject was at the "Coffee Pot" a small restaurant there in Galloway.

Capt. Reed sent Troopers Dosing and Graham to investigate. According to info Capt. Reed obtained the Troopers drove up and were coming in from the rear. Before they reached the door the subject shot through the door and shot Dosing through the head and Graham through the chest. It is unknown just who did what, but when the smoke cleared away Dosing was lying in the door-dead and Milan Nedimovich was also dead. One shot had been fired from Graham's gun and an unknown number of shots (Capt. Reed did not state) had been fired from Dosing's gun. Capt. Reed thinks possibly Dosing did the killing. Nedimovich was in civilian clothes although reported to be in army uniform on item out of Arkansas. Had a Packard car believed to be the one taken at Little Rock.

Margie Smith, who works there at Galloway had been out with Nedimovich last night until three am this date.

She said they had been to Spfd. Also said they planned to get married this afternoon. He is supposed to have been AWOL from Camp Pike since Nov. 30. Gun used is an old Owl Head type 32 Or 38 cal. believed 32.

Graham in St. John's Hospital at Spfd.

Johnson

Author's Note: This message was probably written by Sergeant K. K. Johnson, who was assigned to General Headquarters at the time. The information was very preliminary as it was written only about two hours and fifteen minutes after the shooting. The name of Camp Pike had been changed to Camp Joseph T. Robinson in 1937.

Dosing's body was removed to Herman Lohmeyer Funeral Home in Springfield. Nedimovich's body was not removed until the coroner arrived at the scene. Before the bodies were removed several officers examined the fatal wounds of Dosing and Nedimovich. They also examined damage inflicted by three or four bullets in the door facing, roof, and wall of the upstairs room. They returned that evening to further examine the room.

Early statements initially led investigators to believe the shot fired by Justice Stubbs had killed Nedimovich. But a close examination of Nedimovich revealed a small entry wound with powder burns on the right side of his head. An exit wound on the left side of his head was the size of an egg. An examination of Nedimovich's gun indicated it was a Harrington-Richardson thirty-eight caliber five shot pistol. It was also referred to as an inexpensive "Owls Head" gun. Sergeant Viets examined the weapon and found the hammer was back, but the gun was "jammed," with three rounds still in the weapon. Two rounds had

"Up these stairs to the door at the top of them, State Patrolmen Victor Dosing and Sam Graham walked about noon yesterday—Dosing to his death and Graham to receive serious wounds. The door opens into the room occupied by Margie Smith, on the second floor of the Coffee Pot, on highway 65 south of Galloway. Through it Private Milan J. Nedimovich fired at the two patrolmen." — Springfield Daily News, December 8, 1941

This was the scene at the Coffee Pot Tavern sometime after the shooting which left Trooper Vic Dosing dead and Trooper Sam Graham critically wounded. (Domino Danzero Family Photograph Collection, Special Collections and Archives, Missouri State University)

No. 2
4-13-40.
5-17-39
PI X23159

DEPARTMENT OF COMMERCE
BUREAU OF THE CENSUS

MISSOURI STATE BOARD OF HEALTH
STANDARD CERTIFICATE OF DEATH

WRITE PLAINLY—USE UNFADING BLACK INK—MAKE A PERMANENT RECORD

JAN 16 1942
Registration District No. 321.

Primary Registration District No.

State File No.

Register's No. 30

41835

1. PLACE OF DEATH:
(a) County: GREENE
(b) City or town: Community Rural Clay Township
(c) Name of hospital or institution: Coffee Pot Inn U.S. Highway 65
(d) Length of stay: In this community: 10 Years   In hospital or institution:

2. USUAL RESIDENCE OF DECEASED:
(a) State: Missouri   (b) County: Greene
(c) City or town: Springfield
(d) Street No.: 954 Kingsbury
(e) If foreign born, how long in U.S.A.?

3. (a) PRINT FULL NAME: Victor Orville Dosing
(b) If veteran, name war: no

4. Sex: Male   5. Color or race: White   6. (a) Single, widowed, married, divorced: Married
(b) Name of husband or wife:
(c) Age of husband or wife if alive:

7. Birth date of deceased: Aug. 21, 1907

8. AGE: Years 34   Months 3   Days 6

9. (a) Birthplace: Bonne Terre, Missouri

10. Usual occupation: Highway Patrolman
11. Industry or business: State of Missouri

12. Name: Martin Dosing
13. Birthplace: Bonne Terre, Missouri
14. Maiden name: Ona Abelle
15. Birthplace: Bonne Terre, Missouri

16. (a) Informant: Mrs. M. Rosalie Dosing
(b) Address: Springfield, Mo.

17. (a) Burial, cremation, or removal: Burial   (b) Date thereof: Dec. 10 1941
(c) Place of burial or cremation: Maple Park

18. (a) Signature of funeral director: H.H. Lohmeyer
(b) Address: Springfield, Mo.

19. (a) Date received for local registration: 1-10-1941

20. DATE OF DEATH: Month Dec. day 7 year 1941 hour 15 min. P.M.

21. I hereby certify that I

MEDICAL CERTIFICATION

22. If death was due to external causes, fill in the following:
(a) Accident, suicide, or homicide (specify):
(b) Date of occurrence:
(c) Where did injury occur?
(d) Did injury occur in or about home, on farm, in industrial place, in public place?

This is a copy of Vic Dosing's death certificate

been fired from it. It became quite evident that Nedimovich had picked up Dosing's gun and had used the only expended round to kill himself.

The investigation continued with the troopers and sheriff talking to the participants involved in the shooting, and the witnesses. Sheriff Wommack and Prosecuting Attorney Collison obtained a written statement from Margie Smith, and Sergeant Viets talked to Trooper Graham at St. John's Hospital. Nedimovich's finger and palm prints were taken and forwarded to Little Rock, Arkansas police.

Test bullets were fired from the guns used by Nedimovich, Constable Love, and Justice Stubbs and taken to the Patrol's General Headquarters in Jefferson City. They were compared with the bullets removed from the body of Earnest Newman. The test was inconclusive and General Headquarters requested that Nedimovich's gun be taken to Jefferson City so that a test bullet could be fired from all five cylinders.

An inquest was held by Acting Coroner G. H. Boehm on December 8 at 2:00 PM. He and Greene County Assistant Prosecuting Attorney E. Andrew Carr questioned the eight witnesses. Constable Love, Justice Stubbs, Margie Smith, Trooper Barkley, Sheriff Wommack, Sergeant Viets, U. R. Coble, and Lela Nix testified after the coroner's jury had viewed the bodies of Vic Dosing and Milan Nedimovich at Herman Lohmeyer Funeral Home.

At the conclusion of the inquest the jury ruled "We, the jury, have come to a decision that Vic Dosing came to his death by a gunshot fired from the hands of Milan Nedimovich by using a 38 Herrington Richardson revolver." They also found that "the said Milan Nedimovich came to his death by his own hand, self inflicted, using Vic Dosing's 38 Police Special."

On Tuesday, December 9, Virgil Sechler, operator of Oak Grove Lodge, viewed the body of Nedimovich and confirmed that he was the soldier with Earnest Newman early in the morning of November 27 when Newman had stopped for gas. That same day, General Headquarters notified Troop D Headquarters that bullets fired from Nedimovich's gun were a positive comparison with those removed from Earnest Newman's body.

Little Rock police asked the service station attendant, who had serviced the stolen Packard the night John Hoffman was killed, to view a photograph of Nedimovich. He was identified as the soldier with the bloody uniform who was driving the Packard.

Herman Lohmeyer Funeral Home contacted Tony Nedimovich, the father of Milan Nedimovich, attempting to learn what he wanted to do with his son's body. The funeral home received a reply by telegram on December 8 from Tony Nedimovich of Eveleth, Minnesota. It stated, "You killed my son and he killed one of you I disown him and will not have anything to do with him dead." He was buried December 16 at Hazelwood Cemetery in Springfield.

On December 31 the Greene County Court paid the funeral home thirty dollars from the General Revenue Fund for the burial of Nedimovich.

CHAPTER TWO

THE DOSING FUNERAL AND PATROL ASSISTANCE FOR HIS FAMILY

FUNERAL SERVICES FOR VIC Dosing were held at 3:00 PM December 10 at the Herman Lohmeyer Funeral Home. An honor guard of troopers stood at the casket for twenty-four hours preceding the service. The service was attended by fifty-two troopers, twenty-two Springfield police officers, and about thirty officers from other police agencies in southwest Missouri. A total of about four hundred people were in attendance. He was buried in Maple Park Cemetery in Springfield.

"All twenty-five members of Troop D of the highway patrol and representatives from every troop in the state attended funeral services for Trooper Vic Dosing yesterday afternoon in Herman Lohmeyer chapel. Some of the troopers wept openly, others were sad-eyed—all mourning the loss of Trooper Dosing, who was killed Sunday in a gun battle with Milan Nedimovich, suspected slayer of two men. Leading the casket (above) are the two officiating ministers. Left is Dr. B. Locke Davis, right, the Rev. Barton A. Johnson. Of Trooper Dosing, Doctor Davis said: "Fellow officers credit him with fearless work and say he was ready and willing at all times to answer the call of duty." Mr. Johnson read scriptures. Behind Doctor Davis, front to rear, are Sergt. O. L. Viets, Trooper Hybert Brooks, and Trooper W. E. Grammer. Fol-

*lowing Mr. Johnson, same order, are Sergt. G. B. Kahler, Trooper
E. B. Burnam, and Trooper H. L. George. Behind the casket is
the guard of honor, Trooper Boyd Robertson, left and Trooper
H. P. Bruner."*

—(Springfield Leader and Press, *December 11, 1941)*

After the death of Vic Dosing his family was making arrangements with Herman Lohmeyer Funeral Home for the service and burial. But the Missouri State Highway Patrol interceded. The Patrol had been in existence only ten years but even then it obviously was an extremely proud organization. That trait has not changed over the years. The troopers today have the same pride in their organization. They are proud to be a member of the Patrol, proud to wear the uniform, proud of the history of those members who served before them, and proud to represent and serve the citizens of Missouri. That amount of pride and strong sense of loyalty to the organization developed into the strong tradition of "Taking care of your own." That tradition is evident in almost all police agencies.

Some of the desire to help and to "Take care of your own" might have originated following the shooting death of Sergeant Ben Booth at Columbia on June 14, 1933, the first trooper killed in the line of duty. The Patrol was in its infancy. The troopers had been patrolling the highways for only one and one-half years. Sergeant Booth was survived by his wife and two small children. It is not known how the members of the Patrol might have assisted her financially, but there were no death benefits and Alice Booth was at least partially responsible for the funeral expenses. It was many years before she was able to finish paying for those funeral expenses.

The members of the Patrol were determined to help Rosalie Dosing and her daughters. Colonel M. Stanley Ginn organized the campaign to pay for the funerals of Troopers Fred Walker and Vic Dosing. Walker had died on December 3, 1941, after being shot the day before near Bloomsdale in St. Genevieve County.

Colonel Ginn asked each trooper and radio operator to contribute to both the Walker and Dosing funeral expenses. Trooper Walker's amount was less than Dosing's because Walker had no dependents. Colonel Ginn wanted a larger contribution to the Dosing fund so that there would be an amount for the benefit of Rosalie and her daughters after the funeral expenses were paid.

December 12, 1941

Mrs. V. 0. Dosing

954 Kingsbury

Springfield, Missouri

Dear Mrs. Dosing:

The members of the Patrol want to pay the funeral expenses, and so arrangements have been made
for the bill at Herman Lohmeyer's, and will be
taken care of through this office, and will be
paid by each of the men in the Patrol.

I explained this to Mr. Dosing, your father-
in-law, when I was there, and while he had
already made arrangements to pay these expenses,
I insisted that the men be permitted to take
care of this item.

In addition to the funeral expenses there
will be some money, although I can't say now
exactly how much, that will be sent to you.

If at any time, there is any way in which we can
be of service to you, please don't hesitate to let

us know your needs. We feel that you and your family are also members of the Patrol, and it would be a genuine pleasure for any man in the department to be at your service.

I just received word that Trooper Graham is in serious condition, and I am considerably worried about him.

I would like to call to see you on my next trip to Springfield.

Sincerely yours,

M. Stanley Ginn

Superintendent

MSG:MS

Jefferson City, Missouri
December 15, 1941

TROOP COMMANDERS

1.   As in previous cases where members of this department have lost their lives, it is contemplated that each member will be asked to contribute to the funeral expenses and family relief of those members.   It has been deemed advisable to pay the funeral expenses for Trooper Fred L. Walker, which amounts to $484.00, and to pay no further benefit since Trooper Walker had no dependents.   This will amount to $3.15 for each remaining member.

2.   For the payment of funeral expenses of Trooper V. 0. Dosing under this plan the allotment for each member will be the sum of $5.00, the balance to be paid to Mrs. Dosing.

3.   It is suggested that these two accounts be handled entirely separate in order that the complete records of each my go in the personnel file of the member so affected.

4.   If at all possible the money should be collected and forwarded to this office for disbursement through the proper channels on or before January 15, 1942.

M. Stanley Ginn
Superintendent

MSG:MS
Copy to
Troop A — B — C — D — E — F - Radio

Jefferson City, Missouri

January 20, 1942

Subject: Dosing Funeral Expenses

            Contributions to Mrs. V. O. Dosing

To: C.O., Troop D

1.   Attached is draft in the amount of $404.00 payable to Herman H. Lohmeyer Funeral Home, Inc., to cover complete funeral expenses of the late Trooper V. O. Dosing.

2.   Draft in the amount of $511.00 to be delivered to Mrs. Dosing is also attached, which is the balance of the contribution made by members of this department.

3 . Acknowledge receipt.

M. Stanley Ginn

Superintendent

MSG:MS

Author's Note: Following is a Patrol Bulletin issued December 12, 1941.

TROOPER

V. O. DOSING

Born August 31, 1907

Appointed October 5, 1931

Killed in line of duty December 7, 1941

The Patrol is again forced to announce with regret that another member has paid the extreme price in the performance of his duty. It is assuring evidence that the caliber of the men with whom we work is such as to justify the confidence we have placed in them, and that the clarion call of duty will forever be met without wavering or hesitation.

From our ranks a new troop is forming, one which draws its membership from those who have been ready to sacrifice all earthly ties in a strict devotion to an ideal, that our society may endure the mutations of time, and the world they left be better than that into which they came. Their memory and their example will continue to exert an influence in the lives of members of the Patrol and friends of our departed officers.

Trooper Dosing's death has had a sobering influence in the minds of all of us. We are again reminded that the call of our profession may sometimes demand this supreme sacrifice. We are powerless to stop the wheel of time and circumstances, and no mortal effort of ours can ever reverse that decision of fate which has deprived us of our fellow trooper. Death, itself, is inescapable, but when it comes it is well to realize that it represents such a direct investment in the benefit of all mankind.

Author's note: On January 27, 1942 Rosalie Dosing wrote the following letter to Colonel Ginn.

Springfield, Mo.

January 27, 1942

Colonel M. Stanley Ginn

Missouri State Highway Patrol

Jefferson City, Missouri

Dear Colonel Ginn:

    I wish to express to you, each officer, and Trooper of the Patrol, my appreciation for your generosity. It is a reminder to me of the loyalness of an organization of which my husband was proud to be a member.

Very Sincerely,

Mrs. V. O. Dosing

May a copy of this be forwarded to each troop.

CHAPTER THREE

QUESTIONS FROM THE RESEARCH

FACT AND DETAIL WILL be used in an attempt to address some of the many questions which developed while researching Dosing's death. But for many reasons already mentioned in the Introduction, fact and detail were almost non-existent at times as I attempted to locate as much information as possible for this book. Much of the response to some of the questions will be almost solely my opinion or speculation. Some of the questions may have no conclusive answer, and may even create additional questions.

Could the shootout have been prevented?

This seems to be the least difficult question to address. Trooper Dosing, John Hoffman of Little Rock, and Ernest Newman of Washington, Missouri would not have been killed, and Trooper Graham would not have been critically wounded, if the wheels of justice had turned differently.

If Jimmy Nedimovich had been imprisoned by either the Army or civilian courts, these three murders would have been avoided. I am not going to suggest that he would not have killed other people in later years, but those three murders would not be a part of history.

Nedimovich was arrested by Constable Love and Justice Stubbs on October 9, 1941 in Galloway in the Buick he admitted stealing in St. Louis. He was AWOL from Ft. Leonard Wood at the time. If he was still in the Army, why was he allowed so much time off the military base? Did the Army discharge him because of the stolen vehicle? If not, is it possible they did not know about the stolen vehicle? When he was arrested, he was held for Ft. Wood on the AWOL offense. Was information about the stolen Buick misplaced or never forwarded to them? That seems highly unlikely. If the Army was aware of the theft, was the usual procedure for such an offense some type of discharge?

If he was discharged, why was he not turned over to St. Louis authorities serving a warrant for prosecution of the auto theft offense? Did the St. Louis Prosecuting Attorney's Office have such a lenient attitude toward auto theft committed by military personnel that there were no charges filed?

Why did the troopers go up the stairs?

It seems there is a correlation between the consideration of this question and the age of the person requesting an answer. As a general rule, a younger reader is more distantly removed in time from the law enforcement methods of seventy years ago, and consequently, not as familiar with what officers faced as they performed their duties.

On December 7, 1941, there were twenty-three troopers working the twenty-two counties which comprised Troop D at that time. Many of the smaller counties had only a sheriff and possibly one deputy. Fulltime law enforcement officers were few in number and they were responsible for enforcement in very large areas. A trooper was accustomed to being "The Man." He normally handled his duties by himself because there were no other options. Normally there would rarely have been more than one trooper on duty for coverage for every two or three counties. If another trooper happened to be as close as twenty or thirty miles and available to assist on a call, the first trooper requesting assistance would have had to locate a telephone, or ask a civilian to find a phone and make a call on his behalf. As a result of the lack of two-way radios and the realization that there would usually be a very lengthy delay before any law enforcement help could arrive, even if other officers could be notified, the troopers were accustomed to acting alone, regardless of the circumstances requiring their attention.

It was a very unusual set of circumstances, which could not have been anticipated by Troopers Dosing and Graham, that allowed four troopers to arrive on the scene ten to fifteen minutes after the shooting, estimated at 12:10 to 12:15 PM. There is no mention of any officer, other than those four troopers, arriving before Sergeant Viets. He was called at home about 12:20 PM by Captain Reed and informed of the shooting. He arrived between 12:30 PM and 12:35 PM. Sheriff Wommack arrived from his home about 12:40 PM. The fact that Sergeant Viets and Sheriff Wommack were called from home and were the first local officers to arrive is an indication of how sparsely staffed the state was with law enforcement officers.

Troopers Dosing and Graham planned their actions on the information they possessed at the time. They had been told that a Little Rock murder suspect *might* be at the Coffee Pot Tavern. It is unknown how many details they might have been provided. Could they have been told the Little Rock victim had been beaten to death? If so, they might not have been quite as concerned about the possibility he might be armed with a firearm, with an obvious willingness to use it to avoid arrest. Even if that detail could have been given to them, they would have assumed that he might have had one or more firearms. How many firearms might he have? If he had a firearm, could it be one or more handguns, or even a rifle or shotgun? There is no indication they were aware Margie Smith was in the room with him. Sergeant Viets, in his report, indicates that Justice Stubbs told him Mrs. Coble informed Constable Love and him that the Packard parked behind the building belonged to Nedimovich and he was upstairs with Margie Smith.

What were their options for investigating the possibility that a murder suspect was at the Coffee Pot? When they arrived, there was no option about entering the building. They could not discretely call by telephone and ask the person who answered if Nedimovich was on the premises. There was no telephone. If he was indeed at that location, he was probably in the tavern. They went in the front door and when it was apparent Nedimovich was not in the room, they asked U. R. Coble where he was. Coble replied that Nedimovich was upstairs. When asked how they could get upstairs, Coble told them to go out the rear kitchen door and up the stairs. They immediately started through the kitchen. It was obvious that they were trying to get upstairs as quickly as possible because Constable Love did not catch them until they were going out the kitchen door. I would speculate that their strategy was to attempt to surprise Nedimovich and eliminate as much time as possible that he might have to plan any actions against them, if he desired.

Another option would have involved asking everyone in the downstairs portion of the building to leave, and then watching the stairway to the room upstairs while someone went to a phone to call for additional help. It would probably have taken an hour for several officers to be summoned and drive to the scene. A hostage standoff would likely have resulted. Again, they had no idea what kind of weapons and ammunition Nedimovich might have in the room. They may have been able to communicate with him by yelling (the only method of communication available to them). But, in hindsight, Nedimovich was determined to die rather than be taken into custody. Would he have used Margie Smith as a shield to exit down the stairs? What would have been the result of that action? How many officers would he have attempted to kill? Would he have killed Margie? What if he had been armed with additional handguns?

If the troopers had elected to leave the building and a standoff followed, how many hours or days would they have waited before they took action? What action would they have taken? It is not known if the Patrol was equipped with tear gas guns at that time or if the sheriff might have had one.

If a gas gun had been available and used, would Nedimovich have exited shooting his way down the stairs, or would he have exited using Margie as a shield? If a gas gun had not been available, or if the decision was made for the troopers to go up the stairs, what would the outcome have been?

It is my opinion the troopers took the most prudent course of action. They were accustomed to acting alone and efficiently. They did not have the time or resources to handle complications. In this instance two troopers were a powerful force not normally seen in an enforcement encounter. They probably just wanted to determine if Nedimovich was indeed the Little Rock murder suspect, and, if not, to continue with their other duties.

Was Trooper Dosing shot because he was already familiar to Nedimovich? Dosing (probably accompanied by Graham) had transported him to jail following his arrest two months earlier (October 9) by Constable Love and Justice Stubbs for investigation of auto theft and AWOL.

It seems highly unlikely that the identity of the officers climbing the stairs to the room occupied by Nedimovich and Margie Smith influenced the decision-making of Nedimovich. He had beaten John Hoffman to death in Little Rock about thirty-six hours earlier. The Packard he had stolen from that murder scene was parked behind the Coffee Pot. He knew he was in a situation from which he could not easily escape. He would be arrested for murder, unless he eliminated the officers there to arrest him. He would not hesitate to kill to keep from being arrested for murder. In his demented mind, the possibility of being arrested for murder was a much greater reason to kill than that which had compelled him to kill his first two victims, Ernest Newman for a car and thirty-five dollars, and John Hoffman for a car.

I am convinced Nedimovich would have shot any officers climbing the stairs, regardless of their names or the organization they represented.

What was status of Milan Nedimovich with the U.S. Army?

This question still cannot be answered with certainty. The July 12, 1973 fire at the National Personnel Records Center in St. Louis destroyed at least sixteen million military files, including those of Milan James Nedimovich. Inquiry revealed there were no records at Fort Leonard Wood or Camp Robinson. *The Eveleth News* reported on December 11, 1941 that "Nedimovich was inducted into the United States army as a selective service trainee on July 18 (1941) and that no local information is available as to when and if he was discharged from the military forces." If his Army records were available it could be determined when his basic training at Fort Leonard Wood was completed, when he transferred to Camp Robinson, if he was in confinement following the AWOL offense and stolen vehicle arrest at Galloway (Margie did not see him for about one month following his arrest), and his status at the time of his death.

Following the Coffee Pot shooting most of the Springfield newspaper accounts referred to Nedimovich as "ex-soldier" or "former soldier." Some of the newspaper accounts in Springfield, Washington, and Cassville, Missouri, and Little Rock, Arkansas, all places where his three victims had lived, referred to him as an AWOL soldier or deserter. One Little Rock newspaper even suggested that he had been transferred to Camp Robinson but had never reported for duty there. That account was certainly inaccurate because he had received letters from Margie Smith addressed to him at Camp Robinson.

Army officials sent a telegram to Greene County officials asking that the body of Nedimovich be held until it could be identified by Army officials. In the afternoon of December 12, Second Lieutenant B. W. Ryden of Fort Leonard Wood identified the body. The *Springfield*

Daily News reported that Ryden said Nedimovich had been AWOL one time while under his command at Fort Leonard Wood. If Nedimovich had been discharged from the Army, would Army officials have asked to identify his body after his death?

After the death of John Hoffman in Little Rock the night of December 5 and the discovery that the killer was wearing a bloodied Army uniform when he obtained fuel for the stolen car, Little Rock police asked Camp Robinson officials for information on AWOL soldiers. Camp Robinson provided the name of Claudie D. Davis, who, like Nedimovich, had previously been stationed at Fort Leonard Wood. The fact that Nedimovich's name was not provided, along with that of Davis, could be interpreted as evidence that Nedimovich was no longer in the military.

If Nedimovich had not been discharged, was he on leave or AWOL? Margie Smith said in her statement the she had seen him for varying lengths of time on November 23, 24, 25, 26, 29, 30 and December 1, 2, 6, and 7. If he had not been discharged, would he have had that much leave time?

The most definitive information about his status came from the comments of Constable Love reported by the *Springfield Daily News* on December 8, 1941. Love told the newspaper representative that he and Justice Stubbs had arrested Nedimovich in the stolen Buick on October 6. Love said Nedimovich "admitted stealing the car from a used car lot in St. Louis, and it's still in Galloway. We turned him over to the highway patrol. They had been hunting him on an AWOL order from Fort Wood, and they told us they had turned him over to the military police from Camp Robinson. (Author's note: jail records indicate he was released to Fort Leonard Wood authorities.) We thought he'd get at least a year, but we found out later he had just been discharged from the army. If the army had done what it should have done then, all this might not have happened today," said Love bitterly. "Imagine just turning loose a red-hot like that."

Why did James Nedimovich abandon Ernest Newman's body and vehicle at the locations he chose?

This question cannot be answered by me. I have included this information solely for the reader's speculation, if he or she wishes, just as I have devoted many hours to speculation on this topic.

Newman's body and his vehicle were found at different locations about eight miles southwest of Waynesville. Waynesville is just west of Fort Leonard Wood and about eighty miles east of Springfield. Newman's car and body were found about fifty-five to sixty miles from the Oak Grove Lodge. For some time I had thought Nedimovich was still stationed at Fort Leonard Wood when Newman was killed. With the absence of military records, it was easy to make that assumption. It was some time before I noticed the November 6 date on a letter Margie Smith wrote to him at Camp Robinson. He had obviously been transferred to Camp Robinson before that date.

Newman would have been westbound on Highway 66 when he was driving from his home at Washington, Missouri to his parent's home at Cassville. He would have passed Fort Leonard Wood and Waynesville. Somewhere along that route, and before he reached the Oak Grove Lodge east of Strafford, he would have encountered Nedimovich, who was in uniform and probably hitch-hiking.

Margie Smith's statement indicated Nedimovich had left her about 1:30 PM on November 26. He had said he was returning to Camp Robinson. If her statement was correct, Nedimovich would have traveled northeast toward Fort Leonard Wood rather than southeast in the direction of Little Rock. He would have been given a ride by Ernest Newman no more than fourteen hours later.

Nedimovich saw Margie Sunday through Wednesday, leaving that afternoon, November 26. He was with Newman early the next morning. Had he already been discharged from the Army? If not, did he really have that much free time during the week? Why did he go toward Fort Leonard Wood instead of Camp Robinson when leaving the Coffee Pot?

Some investigation reported in the newspaper indicated the approximate number of miles Newman's car would have traveled from his home to the Oak Grove Lodge, and then east again to the site where it was abandoned, was up to fifty miles less than service records for Newman's car indicated it had been driven. If that assessment was correct, where had the car been driven?

A continuation westbound to the Coffee Pot would have accounted for those possibly missing miles. But Nedimovich would have had to kill Newman and put his body in the trunk to complete a visit to Margie or even spend some time in Springfield. In Margie's statement, if completely accurate, she said she did not see Nedimovich from 1:30 PM on Wednesday until about 9:30 PM on Saturday, November 29.

Why did the westbound Nedimovich go back east nearly sixty miles to dispose of Newman and his car after kidnapping or killing him?

Was Margie Smith aware of her boyfriend's criminal activities?

This question is entertained by almost everyone who has any knowledge of the Coffee Pot shooting and the criminal history of Milan Nedimovich. There was no mention in the law enforcement reports of any suspicion that Margie was aware of either of Nedimovich's other murders or the Buick he stole in St. Louis. None of the newspaper accounts suggest that she had knowledge of those other incidents.

She authored an article that appeared in a publication of unknown title. In that article she explained that she had no idea that Nedimovich was anything other than the handsome and personable soldier she had fallen in love with. Many people had apparently asked her if she didn't "think it strange that a mere private was able to drive a Buick Eight coach, even if a 1937 Model," and if she didn't ever have any suspicions about Nedimovich. Her reply to the questions was, "I can only answer: I was a girl who had fallen for her date—hard. And when, since the beginning of time, has an infatuated girl taken time or trouble to think?"

She knew that she would not see him as often after his transfer to Camp Robinson from Fort Leonard Wood because of the much greater distance for him to drive to Springfield. She also feared that the transfer was an indication that he was more likely to eventually be involved in combat in the inevitable war.

There is no question she was completely absorbed with her relationship with Nedimovich. Apparently, because of her concentration on Nedimovich and the progression of their romance, she did not allow herself to objectively process several indications that there might be a more sinister side of Nedimovich. Some of those known indicators and his false statements to her will be addressed.

When Margie first met Nedimovich, he told her that his name was "Jimmie Donnahue." Margie did not see him from about October 9, when Nedimovich was arrested by Constable Love and Justice Stubbs for AWOL and theft of the Buick, until the first part of November. It was only then that he told her his real name, explaining that he used the fictitious name because of a problem with a former girlfriend.

That period of absence was probably the result of disciplinary action following the AWOL offense. He was likely either in confinement or confined to the base. He was also transferred to Camp Robinson during that time. He apparently had written to her and said he was at Scott Field in Illinois. In her November 6 letter to him at Camp Robinson she told him she was hopeful that he would deny something she believed he did not know she was aware of. A few lines later she wrote, "Darling, you weren't at Scott Field at all were you?" Could she have learned that he really did not go to Scott Field without also learning that he had been arrested?

For at least one month after they began dating, he drove the three-year-old Buick that he had stolen in St. Louis. Then he drove a motorcycle at least one time and apparently hitchhiked several times to visit her until December 6, when he arrived in the stolen Packard from the murder scene in Little Rock.

Margie testified at the coroner's inquest that sometimes Nedimovich had money, and at other times he did not. He had explained that the amount of money he had varied with his pay checks. They had planned to get married a week after the Coffee Pot shooting. She was asked if he had money for their wedding trip to Florida. She indicated that he did not, and said that she had asked him what money they were going to use to finance their trip to Florida. He had replied that he had left the army and was going to get a bonus the next week.

Nedimovich arrived at the Coffee Pot about 10:30 PM on December 6. He and Margie left about 11:45 PM after she got off work. She said they drove to Gilmore's first, stayed about forty-five minutes, and then went to the Oasis. They stayed a short time and then "came back up town." She made that statement at the coroner's inquest held at 227 East Olive in Springfield, not far from the square. With her comment that they "Came back up town," she was obviously referring to the area near the square. They arrived back at the Coffee Pot about 3:30 AM. The period of time that they would have been in the area of the square would have possibly been 2:00 AM to 3:15 AM.

Early in the morning of December 7, Springfield police officer John Rollins followed a car with an Arkansas license plate eastbound on St. Louis Street, which runs east from the square. He first began following it at Kimbrough, which is about three blocks east of the square. The car traveled a few blocks and pulled into a service station briefly, and then went another few blocks before pulling into another service station. He thought the driver was probably looking for a place to air a tire. It was occupied by a young couple. He did not stop the vehicle but, after he became aware of the Coffee Pot shooting later in the day, he was relatively certain he had followed Nedimovich's vehicle.

Following the shooting it was determined by motor number that the Packard at the Coffee Pot was the stolen vehicle from Little Rock. Sergeant Viets' report indicated that the Arkansas license, 41-212, was no longer on the Packard. It had been replaced with a license, 770-417, the owner said had been stolen the night of December 6. The report did not specify which state had issued the stolen plate.

If it was indeed Nedimovich's vehicle that officer Rollins observed closely for some time on St. Louis Street, one could make the assumption that Nedimovich was well aware of the attention he had received from a police officer and decided to replace the stolen Arkansas plate on the stolen vehicle he was driving. If that was the case, he would almost certainly have stolen a license from a state other than Arkansas. He was in Springfield, Missouri and a Missouri plate would have been the least conspicuous.

Research of antique vehicle license plates on the internet revealed that in 1941, all three of the Arkansas plates that were found were five number plates. Of the five Missouri plates found, three were six number and two were five number plates.

If Springfield officer Rollins had indeed been following the stolen Packard occupied by Nedimovich and Margie Smith, the stolen six digit plate would have been placed on the Packard between the time it was observed by Officer Smith and the arrival of Nedimovich and Margie Smith at the Coffee Pot about 3:30 AM. If this information is correct, Nedimovich might have stolen the plate before he and Margie left the Coffee Pot at 11:30 PM. But, Margie would have been with him when he attached the stolen plate to the car. The one reason that she might not have known about the stolen plate would have been if she had briefly removed herself from the area of the vehicle. If that was the case, could she have made a visit to a restroom?

I was hesitant at first to include the previous few paragraphs concerning Nedimovich and Margie's trip to town the night of December 6 because it might suggest Margie had knowledge of, and was possibly complicit in, the theft of the license plate. But I decided those reading this book have the right to read all the information that could be obtained. I am not attempting to implicate Margie Smith in anything that was not proper and legal. I am only reporting a set of circumstances that drew my interest. It is only a possibility that the events and speculation reported above actually occurred.

Margie Smith was admittedly very much in love and infatuated with Milan Nedimovich. Her thinking was consumed with thoughts of him and their future. It seems that she was also very naïve. But there is no indication that she had any knowledge of Nedimovich's homicidal mind and could not have done anything to prevent the murders.

What happened to Margie Smith?

One of Margie Smith's nephews stated that she had been killed in an auto accident in 1954 or 1955. That accident was not located in Missouri. She had married but did not have children.

Trooper Vic Dosing, badge number 22.

CHAPTER FOUR

TROOPER VICTOR ORVILLE DOSING

VICTOR ORVILLE DOSING WAS born August 1, 1907 at Bonne Terre, in St. Francois County, Missouri. He was the oldest son of Martin and Ona Aberley Dosing. His father was a shop teacher at Flat River High School. A younger brother, Elmo James Dosing, was born May 1, 1923.

Vic graduated from Flat River High School in 1926, attended the University of Alabama for one year in 1926-1927, where he studied chemical engineering, played football, and was a member of the R.O.T.C. unit. His brother became very ill in Texas while Vic was in Alabama. After that first year in college Vic moved to Texas to be with his family while Elmo was receiving medical care. Following Elmo's recovery the family moved back to Missouri where Vic enrolled at Flat River Junior College. After two years he received his Associate of Arts degree.

He then enrolled at Central Methodist College at Fayette, Missouri. From 1929 to 1931 he was a member of the Missouri National Guard and, from June through September of 1930, he was in the Army as a flying cadet. He was also a member of the Central Methodist College football team. During the summers of 1928 through 1931 he worked as a clerk at the National Hotel in Flat River, Missouri. He graduated with a Bachelor of Arts degree in May, 1931 and began employment as a carpenter with Titanium Pigment Company in St. Louis.

Vic began dating Rosalie Settle of Fayette while he was a student at Central Methodist College. On May 10, 1931 they were married in a

Troop Meeting January 15, 1933 at Log City on Highway 66 in Jasper County. The original nine troopers assigned to Troop D are shown from the left: Harve Sayers, George Kahler, John Soraghan, Walt Grammer, Charles Newman, Captain L. E. Eslick, O. L. Viets, Vic Dosing, and H. L. George. Additional troopers are Hub Wells and Chet Oliver.

appointment and received a salary set by statute "not to exceed eighteen hundred dollars per year."

Vic was one of the fifty-one original members of the Patrol. They completed six weeks of training at the St. Louis Police Academy and were then given a week to make arrangements at their new troop assignments. Vic did exceptionally well at the Academy, finishing fourth in the class. On November 23 the new members assembled at Jefferson City for their final instructions. On the following day they began patrolling the highways for the first time.

Vic and Oliver Viets were two of nine original members assigned to Troop D. They lived in Sringfield. The original Troop D Headquarters was located in the Missouri State Highway Department District Office in Joplin. The headquarters was moved in May, 1933 to the Highway Department Office at 923 North Weller in Springfield. That building now houses the offices of the Springfield-Greene County Park Board. In 1948 Troop D moved into a new headquarters at the southwest corner of Fremont and Seminole. A portion of that building still remains as part of the Ray Kelly Senior Center. In 1948 another move was made into a new building on West Sunshine. Finally, in February, 1977 Troop D Headquarters moved for the last time to 3131 East Kearney in Springfield.

Author's Note: In the picture at left two of the troopers have their Sam Browne belts worn over the right shoulder instead of the left shoulder and did not have a holstered weapon, Captain Eslick in the center and Trooper Sayers on the far left. Sayers may have been a sergeant at that time. In the picture of the casket of Trooper Dosing being carried from the funeral chapel, the troopers carrying the casket had the Sam Browne belt over the right shoulder without a weapon. The two honor guard members had the Sam Browne belt over the left shoulder with the holstered revolver. Also, some of the pictures of the original class at the state capital indicate the captains had the Sam Browne belt over the right shoulder with no weapon. This was obviously a custom practiced at more formal events. After the rank of sergeant was established, some pictures also indicated both captains and sergeants wore the Sam Browne reversed. I have not learned the origin of the custom or how long after the Dosing funeral it was practiced.

This picture was also taken January 15, 1933. Vic Dosing is standing beside his Patrol motorcycle closest to the camera.

On January 14, 1933 the Dosings became the parents of their first daughter, Jo Ann, who was born with a dislocation of both hips.

On July 12, 1934 Vic submitted a request to the Superintendent for a temporary transfer to Troop C for ninety days beginning July 15. His request was based on the desire to be with Jo Ann when she had "a very delicate and dangerous operation which can be done only by a surgeon who specializes in bone surgery." He added that only a few surgeons in the state could perform the needed operation. Dr. Klinefeller of St. Louis was one of those. Jo Ann would need treatment for several months at the hospital. He said the cost of Rosalie living in St. Louis while he stayed in Springfield would be a financial burden and he strongly desired to be with his family during the hospital stay.

The transfer request was approved with the stipulation that a Troop C trooper temporarily transfer to Troop D for a corresponding period of time so manpower levels would not be affected.

Jo Ann apparently recovered from the surgery and progressed very well in her treatment because Vic was transferred back to Springfield after one month. Jo Ann's recovery required that she wear a body cast for one and one-half years. It was a difficult time for the Dosing family. It was routine for Vic to carry little Jo Ann around in her body cast.

A second daughter, Janet Lee, was born May 1, 1939.

On April 27, 1941 he was returning to Springfield from Jefferson City on his Patrol motorcycle. Between Eldon and Bagnell Dam he was following another vehicle which had to slow to avoid a third vehicle that pulled onto the road in front of it. Vic applied the brake but the road had been freshly oiled and the motorcycle slid causing him to have to lay it down. It suffered minor damage but Vic's new breeches and shirt were damaged beyond repair.

He applied for reimbursement of the cost of replacing the breeches and shirt. The request was granted and he was paid $15.50 for replacement of the breeches and $9.50 for the shirt from the Highway Patrol Benefit Fund.

This is a Troop D troop meeting picture taken in 1936. In the front row from the left are Trooper Burnum, Troop Sergeant Sayers, Sergant Viets, Sergeant Newman, Troopers Kahler, George, and Oliver. In the back row from the left are Troopers Graham, Wright, Grammer, Eidson, Dosing, Brooks, and McClure.

After the incident mentioned above involving an accident on his Patrol motorcycle, it would not be difficult to believe the smile displayed by Vic was an indication he preferred the safety and security of riding the photography studio horse, rather than his Patrol motorcycle.

Troopers did not receive an increase in the base salary of one hundred and fifty dollars a month until 1945. That increase was fifty dollars a month. Vic had received a second increase in pay on October 5th, 1941. The first increase was nine dollars and thirty cents. The 1941 increase elevated his monthly salary to one hundred seventy-five dollars and forty-five cents. Those raises were apparently longevity increases.

Jack McDowell was sixteen years of age when Vic Dosing was killed. Jack's father, Walter, had opened McDowell's Service Station in Strafford in 1924. Jack McDowell was well acquainted with Vic. He described Vic as "a nice guy, friendly, and liked by everyone." He added that Vic had a lot of energy.

Retired Sergeant H. P. Bruner and retired Lieutenant E. B. Burnam worked with Vic. They were all good friends. Both described Vic as a dedicated and hardworking trooper. He associated well with people and was aggressive in handling his duties.

Jo Ann remembered the scream from her mother when Dr. Johnson and others notified Rosalie in another room of Vic's death. The

death of Vic Dosing left his family in a very difficult set of circumstances. Rosalie had two young daughters, and a third, Vicki, was born
eleven weeks later, February 22, 1942. She was not employed and had
not received any type of specialized training. The money given her by
the members of the Patrol helped, and Vic's parents assisted in many
ways. Rosalie's mother stayed with the family for a period of time.

Rosalie decided to acquire specialized training for future employment. She attended Draughon's Business College for training in stenography. That training could only be accomplished with help from
others in taking care of her three young daughters. Her mother moved
in for a time following the death of Vic. Jo Ann stayed with her Dosing
grandparents and rode the train from St. Louis to Springfield to visit on
weekends, and then returned to St. Louis on Sundays. For a time Janet
and Vicki stayed with a couple in north Springfield.

When Rosalie completed her stenography training she was
employed by Troop D Headquarters of the Patrol on September 1, 1942
to fill a position on the clerical staff. She retired November 1, 1966.

This picture was taken in 1946 at Troop D Headquarters. Rosalie Dosing has her back to
the camera and Betty Stafford is facing the camera.

Rosalie remarried for a time but that marriage did not last. She was divorced and again assumed the Dosing name. Rosalie passed away February 1, 1981 and was buried beside Vic in Maple Park Cemetery in Springfield.

This picture of the Troop D office personnel was taken in 1963. Front row left to right: Gayla Burlison (later Harper), Delena Snider, and Joan Seiner. Second row: Ruth Harris, Rosalie (Dosing) Phelps, and June Sullins.

Author's note: This picture is a reminder of two of the tragic sacrifices of troopers and their families. Rosalie Phelps was the widow of Trooper Vic Dosing. Gayla Burlison would many years later marry Trooper Russell Harper and also became a widow when he was killed by a burst of fire from an automatic weapon on February 8, 1987, forty-five years following the murder of Vic Dosing. Trooper Harper was killed in Greene County on U. S. 60 about one mile east of U. S. 65. That location is about two miles from the site of the Coffee Pot Tavern before it burned.

This picture was taken in 1966 at Troop D Headquarters. The occasion was obviously a celebration honoring the retirement of Rosalie (Dosing) Phelps. Rosalie Phelps is in the center of the picture facing the camera. There is a cake on the far table and a note written on the chalkboard, "Thank you Rosie." Gayla Burlison (later Harper) is also in this picture, on the far right. Rosalie's daughters, Jo Ann and Janet, are two of the ladies with their backs to the camera. Her retirement date was November 1, 1966.

The tombstone for Vic and Rosalie Dosing in Springfield's Maple Park Cemetery.

Jo Ann Dosing graduated from Central High School in Springfield in 1950. She worked in the medical field and retired in Florida. She had two daughters and a son. One daughter died at an early age and her son was named Victor. She said on several occasions that she dearly loved the Patrol and that if women had been allowed to become troopers, she would have cherished the opportunity to follow her father as a member. Janet Lee Dosing is married and living near Springfield. She has two daughters and is retired from a career as a travel agent. Vicki Ona Dosing never married and lives in Arizona. She is retired following a career as a lab technician.

Trooper Samuel S. Graham

CHAPTER FIVE

TROOPER SAMUEL STANLEY GRAHAM

SAMUEL STANLEY GRAHAM WAS born March 5, 1912 at Smithfield, Missouri to Stanley J. and DeEtta McBee Graham. Smithfield is a village in the western edge of Jasper County, Missouri, just west of Carl Junction.

He attended school at Smithfield through the eighth grade and graduated from high school in Joplin, Missouri in 1929. He was employed by an auto dealer for one year as a mechanic, and then enrolled at Kansas State College in Pittsburg for one year, where he took classes in chemistry and mathematics. He then worked again for about two years for the auto dealer as a parts man. For much of 1933 and 1934 he was an engineer's chain man. He was then laid off and apparently became a casualty of the Great Depression for several months.

He mailed an employment application to the Missouri State Highway Patrol, which was received by the Patrol on March 18, 1935. Sam declared himself to be a Democrat. He was given a physical examination on June 25, 1935 in Jefferson City. He also appeared before an interview board comprised of nine men and

This is a Troop D troop meeting picture taken in 1937 or the first part of 1938. It was taken outside the District Highway Department Headquarters in Springfield. The Patrol used that building as a troop headquarters until 1938 when they moved into the first new troop headquarters. The troopers wearing the Pershing-style caps were members of the recruit class of 1937. Trooper Vic Dosing is the third from the left on the front row, and Trooper Sam Graham is the fifth from the left.

probably took his written examination on that same day. His physical examination records indicate he was 5'11" in height and weighed 185 pounds.

One short week later, on July 1, 1935, he had been employed and began his recruit training at Camp Clark, Nevada, Missouri. He completed his training of one month and was given the oath of office on July 31. His salary was one hundred and forty-five dollars a month.

Sam was first assigned at Nevada and transferred to Springfield in 1937 or 1938. Within one year after becoming a trooper he married Ethel B. Parker at Joplin, Missouri. A daughter, Neville Sue, was born January 10, 1938. A son, Michael S., was born March 14, 1946. Another son, Samuel L., was born August 19, 1950.

Trooper Sam Graham is on the left with Trooper Vic Dosing.
The picture was taken in April, 1938.

Sam Graham with daughter Neville,
probably in 1940.

After Sam Graham was wounded at the Coffee Pot, he drove to Gooch's Store in Galloway and called for help. Even though he was severely wounded, he drove back to a location just north of the Coffee Pot and waited for help. When the other troopers arrived he briefed them on the situation at the Coffee Pot and then was apparently transported to St. John's Hospital by a person driving by the scene.

When he arrived at the hospital he was "in severe shock, pulse barely perceptible," and had a "blood pressure systolic 40, diastolic not obtainable, pulse 90, inaccurate because of weakness." He was given morphine and a stimulant, and a blood transfusion was given later in the afternoon.

The transfusion was given directly from Trooper E. B. Burnam. Trooper Burnam retired from the Patrol as a lieutenant. He stated in an interview about ten years ago that Sam Graham had been conscious during the transfusion, but that he did not say anything about the shooting. That transfusion helped save Graham's life as his condition improved somewhat afterward.

It was determined that the bullet had entered Graham's left shoulder, traveled through the deltoid muscle and entered the chest cavity. It penetrated the left lung, diaphragm, and left kidney, lodging in the muscles on the left side of his back.

His condition soon began deteriorating and the medical staff could not stop the bleeding from the kidney. The kidney was removed on December 12 and he was again given a blood transfusion. The blood for the second transfusion was donated by Trooper Russell Burk. Graham was placed in an oxygen tent for twenty-four hours on December 13.

He gradually began feeling better as his wounds healed. He was released from the hospital on December 31 and allowed to return to light duty on February 1.

There was no health insurance for troopers in 1941. Trooper Graham's medical bills were paid from the Highway Patrol Benefit Fund (no longer in existence) following authorization by the Missouri State Highway Commission.

Author's note: The following letter, dated January 26, 1942, was written by Dr. T. E. Ferrell, explaining the treatment of Sam Graham.

T.E. Ferrell, Jr. M. D.

600 MEDICAL ARTS BLDG

SPRINGFIELD, Mo

January, 26, 1942

Re. Sam Graham -Age 30 - White - Male - Married

Occupation - Officer, Missouri Highway Patrol

To Whom It May Concern

The above named patient entered St. John's Hospital by ambulance, December 7, 1941, about 1 p.m. because of a gunshot wound to the chest. Examination of patient in hospital revealed man appearing the stated age, in severe shock, pulse barely perceptible, he was cold, clammy and perspiring, blood pressure systolic not obtainable, pulse 90, inaccurate because of weakness. Morphine and stimulant was given, external heat applied, and patient prepared for transfusion, which was given later in the afternoon. Examination of the chest showed a bullet wound of the left shoulder, ranging downward traversing the deltoid muscle and entering chest cavity. There was evidence of hemorrhage in the left lung by physical and x-ray examination, patient was also spitting blood. Catherized specimen showed pure blood in the urine and the bullet was located by x-ray examination in the left region of the back in the neighborhood of the left kidney. Following the transfusion his condition became more favorable. Blood in the urine also became less. Tetanus and gas bucillus antitoxin given. On December 11 blood reappeared in the urine and bladder filled with blood clots which were partially removed by irrigation. However, it was impossible to stop the bleeding form the left kidney so it was necessary to rem0o9ve [sic] the left kidney on December 12, 1941. Immediately following the operation another transfusion was given. There developed some pulmonary congestion in both lungs, and patient was placed in oxygen tent December 13 for about twenty-four hours. Following the operation his condition was one of gradual improvement until he was discharged from the hospital December 31, 1941. He has been seen in the office Jaanuary 3, 8, 10, 17, and 26, 1942, and shows gradual improvement. In my opinion he will be able to return to light work February 1, 1942. Dr. F. E. Glenn and Dr. Robert Vinyard were called in consultation o [sic] this case and assisted in caring for Graham throughout his stay in hospital.

Diagnosis: Gunshot wound of left chest by 38 caliber bullet, which entered left shoulder, traversed the left lung, the left side of the diaphragm, tore through the left kidney and became embeded in the muscles of the back on the left side.

T. E. Ferrell, M.D.

TEF/AF

Sam Graham reading letters and cards the day before his release from the hospital.

Sam Graham recovered from his physical wounds. Emotionally, however, he would never completely recover. Graham family members indicate he assumed the responsibility for the death of his good friend and fellow trooper, and for his own wounds. He believed that he somehow should have been in a position to prevent the shooting. He apparently did not sleep a complete night the rest of his life without dreams or nightmares about the shootings. Those nightmares were at times accompanied by screams. He was never emotionally free of his tormented memories.

After Sam recovered from his wounds, he attempted to enlist in the military, just as many of the troopers did during World War II. He was disqualified for service because he did not pass the physical examination. One could suspicion that the removal of his kidney following the gunshot wound less than a year earlier would have been reason for the disqualification. He then pursued another option with the federal government. On November 19, 1942 Sam Graham resigned from the Patrol and accepted an appointment as a Secret Service Agent of the Treasury Department. He served several years in that capacity at the White House during President Roosevelt's last term in office. He left the Secret Service just after the death of President Roosevelt.

Sam operated a service station in St. Louis for several years before moving to Joplin, Missouri. He worked for several different employers in that area before he became terminally ill with cancer.

Sam Graham was buried in a Graham family plot in Carl Junction Cemetery,
Carl Junction, Missouri with his parents, brother, and grandparents.

Sam Graham's death certificate indicates he died
December 31, 1956 from Bronchogenic Carcinoma.

CHAPTER SIX

THE DOSING MEMORIAL

DURING THE SPRING OF 2003, members of the Missouri State Highway Patrol's Troop D were completing a physical fitness test that included a one and one-half mile run. The run began at Sequiota Park in the Galloway area of Springfield. The troopers ran on a lengthy asphalt walking and biking trail south along Lone Pine Street, which is the old Highway 65, under US 60, and on to the Springfield Nature Center. Several of the older troopers accumulated at the rear of the group before the run began because they didn't want to hinder the progress of those younger and faster.

The trail passes behind a restaurant at the southwest corner of Lone Pine and Republic Road so closely that one can touch the rear of the building. As the group of slower troopers passed behind the restaurant, one of them asked me if that was the restaurant where the trooper was killed many years ago. The question was directed at me because I had worked the Springfield area for my entire career. I replied that was not the correct location. Early in my career one of the older troopers had directed me to the area where the Coffee Pot had been located. I told the group that the correct Coffee Pot site was probably south where a pet cemetery is now located.

By 2003 a tradition had started that allowed law enforcement officers killed in the line of duty to be honored by having a portion of a highway named for them. That conversation that day led to thoughts of exploring the possibility of requesting that Trooper Vic Dosing be honored in that manner. The problem with that idea was, at that time, there was no high-way passing the location of the old Coffee Pot. A new US 65 had been built in the late 1950's. The old Highway 65 roadway is now Lone Pine Street which ends at the present US 60, James River Expressway.

The plan then evolved to inquire about the feasibility of placing a monument honoring Trooper Dosing on the site of the Coffee Pot. Several of the older residents of the Galloway area were interviewed. Nearly all agreed that the site was in the current pet cemetery, but the opinions of the exact place varied by about one hundred yards.

Further research finally led to the Missouri State Department of Transportation District Headquarters in Springfield. Employees there produced several maps and photographs of the old Highway 65 where the Coffee Pot had been located. MODOT engineers studied the maps and found one drawing that included the Coffee Pot location. It was included with many which were made in the 1950's in the planning phase of the new US 60 – US 65 highway just south of the Coffee Pot location. The drawing indicated a round concrete slab close to the old highway, a graveled parking area behind it, a store close to the small stream and directly west of the slab, and a house southwest of the slab. There was also an aerial photograph of the same area which pictured the round Coffee Pot slab, the gravel drive and parking area, and the store adjacent to the stream and railroad tracks at the west side of the property. There was no question that the drawing and photograph depicted the round concrete floor upon which the old Coffee Pot had been built. The engineers then calculated the distance from the center of the slab on a perpendicular line to the roadway. At that point at the edge of the roadway a measurement was taken to the beginning of the curvature of the inside edge of the roadway. Those calculations deter-mined the exact location of the Coffee Pot site. A measurement from that site to the proposed location of the memorial was determined to be one hundred and forty-four feet.

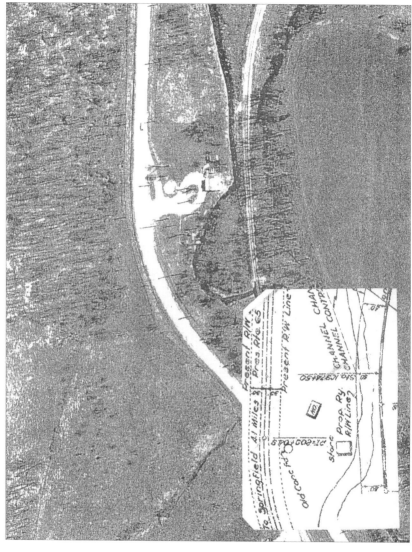

Pictured at right is an aerial photograph of the area of the old Highway 65 and the site of the Coffee Pot Tavern. North is to the left on the picture. Clearly visible is the old Coffee Pot foundation as a white circle. Driveways and the highway are shown as white. The store is very near the bank of the small stream, which is adjacent to the railroad track. The insert is a portion of a drawing by the Missouri Department of Transportation produced in the planning of the new US 65-US 60 highway. It shows "present Rte. 65" and indicates at that time, in the mid-to-late 1950's, it was 4.1 miles to Springfield. Rte. 65 was concrete pavement eighteen feet in width. The right-of-way was thirty feet from the edge of the highway. The round foundation of the old Coffee pot is labeled "Old Concrete Fd." A store is shown at the west side of the property against the railroad right-of-way line and stream.

The pet cemetery was part of Rivermonte Memorial Garden, owned by Thieme-Shadel-Hicks. Jeff and Darla Hicks were part of the ownership team. Mr. Hicks was approached with the idea of placing a memorial monument to Trooper Dosing within the pet cemetery as near as possible to the site of the Coffee Pot. Mr. Hicks was eager to help in any way that he could. Potential locations within the cemetery were studied and an area just off the heavily traveled walking trail and south of the concentration of pet graves was chosen. Mr. Hicks approved the suggestion. The area was measured and found to be one hundred and forty-four feet south of the old Coffee Pot location.

Planning for the monument then began in earnest. Mr. Hicks was very helpful and had many suggestions for the type and size of the monument and the information to be placed on it. The Dosing family offered to pay for the monument but members of the Patrol wanted to "take care of their own." A campaign to raise the money included information sent to all Patrol employees. That information was included in the employees' monthly magazine, the *Patrol News*. In addition, retirees and members of MASTERS (Missouri Association of State Troopers Emergency Relief Society) were also alerted by e-mail. The necessary funds were quickly received and final planning for the content of the monument inscription began.

Again, Mr. Hicks offered many suggestions. Members of the Patrol offered input along with the Dosing family, and the Dosing family made the ultimate decision. The monument was ordered in mid-year, 2004. It was several months before the black granite stone could be quarried and engraved.

Planning then began for the dedication ceremony. Mr. Hicks approved a request for a date of December 7, 2004, at 1:00 PM, the anniversary of the shootings at the Coffee Pot.

Mr. Hicks offered the funeral home facilities for the dedication and he had two canopies erected at the monument. No one was aware that the funeral home was placing a black granite bench with "Dosing" engraved on the front beside the monument. There was no cost for that bench.

Trooper Victor O. Dosing Memorial Dedication

Victor O. Dosing was born August 31, 1907, in Bonne Terre, Missouri. He was the oldest of two sons born to Martin and Ona Aberley Dosing. Victor Dosing graduated from Flat River High School in 1926, where his father was a shop teacher. Victor received an associate of arts degree from Flat River Junior College and a bachelor of arts degree in chemistry from Central Methodist College in May 1931.

On May 10, 1931, Victor married Muriel "Rosalie" Settle from Fayette, Missouri. On January 14, 1933, a daughter, Jo Ann, was born to Victor and Rosalie. On May 1, 1939, a second daughter, Janet Lee, was born.

On October 5, 1931, Victor Dosing was sworn in as an original member of the Missouri State Highway Patrol. Upon graduating from the Academy, he became one of the first two Missouri State Highway Patrol officers assigned to Springfield. Trooper Dosing ranked fourth in his training class. He had a reputation as a skilled investigator. He was described by fellow troopers as fearless and aggressive in his pursuit of criminals. Trooper Dosing also served as a safety officer in the Springfield Public School District.

On Sunday, December 7, 1941, Trooper Victor O. Dosing and Trooper Sam S. Graham responded to the Coffee Pot Tavern in Galloway on U.S. 65 near Springfield. The troopers received information that a Little Rock, Ark., murder suspect may have been staying in a small apartment above the coffee pot-shaped building.

Troopers Dosing and Graham walked up the exterior steps to the second story apartment in an attempt to arrest the suspect. As Trooper Dosing grabbed the doorknob, the door was opened quickly and the suspect fired a shot from a Harrington-Richardson .38 caliber pistol, killing Trooper Dosing instantly. Trooper Graham was critically wounded by a second shot but survived. The suspect retrieved Trooper Dosing's gun and subsequently shot himself to death.

In the aftermath of Victor's murder, the Dosing family tried to pick up the broken pieces of their lives. Rosalie Dosing was pregnant with the Dosing's third child when she was notified of her husband's murder. Vicki Ona, the Dosing's third daughter was born on February 22, 1942. In August 1942, Rosalie Dosing went to work as a stenographer at Troop D Headquarters in Springfield. She worked there for 24 years, retiring on November 1, 1966. She died February 1, 1981. She was buried next to Trooper Dosing in Maple Park Cemetery in Springfield.

Jo Ann Dosing married and had three children. She worked as a physician's assistant and retired to Florida. Janet Lee Dosing married, had two daughters and worked as a travel agent. She remains in the Springfield area. Vicki Ona Dosing lives in Surprise, Ariz., and is a laboratory technician.

The dedication of the memorial marker on December 7, 2004, in honor of Trooper Dosing is a permanent tribute to his sacrifice for the citizens of Missouri.

This handout page was presented to those attending the Dosing Memorial dedication ceremony December 7, 2004.

The dedication was held within the facilities at Rivermonte Gardens, and there were many members of the Patrol, Dosing and Graham family members, officers from other departments, and citizens from the Springfield area present. The Dosing family members had many pictures and mementoes displayed along with a copy of the Springfield newspaper of December 8, 1941, containing articles of the assault on Troopers Dosing and Graham, and of the Japanese attack on Pearl Harbor. Of special interest was the large badge that had been issued to Vic Dosing bearing his badge number "22". In the early days of the Patrol those badges had been worn on the Pershing-style cap. Vic's oldest daughter, Jo Ann, had possession of the badge and she had it beautifully restored. Those large badges are no longer a part of the Patrol uniform.

The ceremony began with the presentation of the colors by the Troop D Honor Guard. Captain John Prine and several others addressed

This is the badge that Vic Dosing wore on his Pershing-style cap. His daughter Jo Ann restored it. His badge number "22" was permanently retired by the Patrol.

the attendees. At the end of the ceremony, Jeff and Darla Hicks, in a hugely generous gesture, presented a check to the Patrol for nearly all of the cost of the monument. That check was subsequently presented to MASTERS. In essence, the Hicks returned the vast majority of the money paid for the monument. The Patrol family, and the families of Troopers Dosing and Graham, will forever be deeply grateful for the eager willingness to help and the "above the call of duty" generosity of Jeff and Darla Hicks.

The ceremony then moved to the pet cemetery where the new Dosing monument had been erected. People were unanimously impressed with the monument. It is an elegant black granite, the picture of Vic Dosing and of the Missouri State Highway Patrol emblem were reproduced very well, and it projects a quiet reverence and sincere appreciation of the sacrifice of Vic Dosing and his family.

The ladies sitting under the shelter are from the left: Vicki, Janet, LaVerne Dosing, widow of Elmo Dosing, only brother of Vic, and Jo Ann. Vicki, Janet, and Jo Ann are the Dosing daughters.

Pictured are Sam Graham and Neville Sue, two of the children of Sam S. Graham.

The Dosing Monument, east side

The Dosing Monument, west side

The Dosing daughters, from left, Janet Lee, Jo Ann, and Vicki Ona are pictured with retired Sergeant Donald Richardson.

Appendix A

PATROL SERGEANT VIETS' REPORT

Troop "D", Springfield, Missouri,

December 15, 1941

Milan James Nedmovitch

Commanding Officer, M.S.H.P., Troop "D",

Springfield, Missouri

1. On Saturday, December 6th, Item #10825 was received from Little Rock, Arkansas, as wanting for murder Claudie D. Davis, 25—5-11—150—a soldier previously stationed at Camp Wood, driving a 39 Metallic colored Packard Coupe, Arkansas 41-212, and that he may come to Missouri.

2. The Springfield Police and Greene County Sheriff's office were called and given the above information.

3. At about 12:20 PM, December 7th, while at home, and just ready to eat lunch, the sheriff called Viets and advised that he believed he just had a good "tip" on the Arkansas car, that he would try to get a little more information and to meet him at his office in about thirty minutes. About ten minutes later Captain Reed called and requested me to go to Galloway at once that he had sent Troopers Dosing and Graham there to investigate a car and had just received a report that both had been shot. When I arrived at Galloway I was informed that

the shooting occurred at the "Coffee Pot", which is a small restaurant and beer parlor, one mile south of Galloway on Route #65. It is built to the shape of a coffee pot and has a one room sleeping room quarters upstairs which is reached by an outside stairway on the west or opposite side of the highway. When I arrived here, Sergeant Wallis, Troopers Brill and Barkley had arrived just ahead of me (they had remained in Springfield returning from Trooper Walker's funeral and had left the office just prior to the call to Captain Reed and were returning to Troop "E"). We were informed that Trooper Graham had been taken to a hospital. In the sleeping room over the Coffee Pot we found Trooper Dosing lying in the door, face down in a large pool of blood, dead. His service pistol was on the floor in front of him. Towards his right with his head against the south wall and also in a large pool of blood and dead was a young man, later learned to be Milan James Nedimovitch. Near his feet was an old type "Harrington-Richard .38 Cal. pistol with the hammer drawn back and apparently "jammed". Both guns were examined and found they had been fully loaded. Dosing's gun had been fired once and the other one twice. At this time the sheriff arrived and was asked to take charge of the guns and all other evidence. Dosing's body was placed in an ambulance and taken to Herman Lohmeyer Funeral Home. The other body was left until the coroner arrived and was then also sent to Herman Lohmeyer.

4. Justice A. F. Stubbs and Constable John Love, both of Galloway, were at the scene and we learned from Stubbs the following: That he and Love received a call from Fat Jones' station which is just south of the Coffee Pot, when they arrived there a man named Stanke from Kansas City and a soninlaw of the man killed at little Rock, Arkansas, was enroute to Little Rock for the funeral and stopped at Jones' station for gas and told Jones

about the incident at Little Rock. Jones told him he believed this 39 Packard may be parked at the Coffee Pot. Stanke got in his car and drove by the Coffee Pot and came back and said he was sure it was his fatherinlaw's car. They then called the constable and justice. Jones then told the justice he believed this was the same man they arrested several months ago for desertion from Camp Wood and had in his possession a stolen car from St. Louis; as he knew that this man was keeping company with Margie Smith who works at the Coffee Pot and rooms upstairs. These officers then called the Patrol office and were told that troopers would be sent. They then drove to the front of the Coffee Pot and inquired of the operator, Mrs. Coble, if the Packard in the back of the place belonged to Nedimovitch. They were told it did and that he and Miss Smith were upstairs. They then drove their car to the back where there is a large parking space so they could watch the stairs and the car and waited for the troopers to arrive. When the troopers arrived they parked in front and apparently went inside and then soon came out of the back door which leads to the stairs and when they started up the stairs the constable called to them to "wait a minute" but apparently they did not hear him and the constable got out his car and followed them upstairs; the justice and Stanke remaining in the car. Dosing was leading and when he arrived about the top step to open the door, the door was jerked open from the inside and he saw a pistol barrel flash and Dosing fell forward into the door, then there was another flash from the inside and Graham started to fall and the constable held him and took him into the back door at the bottom of the stairs. He believes that Graham fired one shot just before or at the time he was struck. At this time it seemed that the door upstairs was wide open and Nedimovitch seemed to start crawling over Dosing's body to come downstairs, then

Stanke handed the justice his gun and said "get him", the justice took the gun (a .38 Cal. Colts revolver) and as he looked up Nedimovitch was standing up a few feet inside the door, and he took deliberate aim and fired and Nedimovitch fell. After Graham and the constable went into the back door, the constable fired several shots out of a south window towards the stairs but the shots were ineffective as the upstairs door cannot be seen from this window. At this time Graham had gone out of the front door to his car and drove to the first station north about ½ mile distant and asked the attendant to call the office and report the shooting; he then drove back to the scene or near there, and parked when a motorist found him and took him to St. john's Hospital. The constable told virtually the same story, as did Margie Smith, except she states that after Nedimovitch shot Dosing and Graham he aimed the gun at her, she screamed and the gun did not go off. He then dropped this gun on the floor and reached for Dosing's gun and then she crouched behind an ironing board and she heard a shot and looked up and he was falling to the floor and lay still. She was held for further questioning.

5. It is believed from all evidence that Nedimovitch, after shooting the troopers, aimed to kill Margie and then himself and when his gun failed or "jammed" he reached for Dosing's gun and the justice believed he was crawling over Dosing's body to come outside and the justice shot a fraction too late, as Nedimovitch had already shot himself. Severe powder burns just over his right ear indicate the gun barrel was against his head when he was shot.

6. Test bullets were fired from the gun in possession of Nedimovitch, the constable's .32 Cal. gun, and the .38 Cal. Colts marked "C.W.T." which was used by the Justice. These specimens were taken to Jefferson City by Captain Shaw, Sergeant Hansen

and Trooper Wells for comparison with the fatal bullets from Ernest Newman's body.

7. The following morning an inquest was held in Judge Boehm's Court and the jury returned a verdict that Trooper Dosing came to his death by gun shot wounds fired by Nedimovitch and that Nedimovitch came to his death by gun shot wounds fired by his own hands from Dosing's gun.

8. At this time General Headquarters advised that the comparison of the fatal bullet was not conclusive and asked that the gun be relayed to Jefferson City for a test bullet to be fired from all five chambers. This evening this Harrington-Richards gun was taken by Captain Reed, Sergeant Kahler and Trooper Grammer to Junction #64 and #73 where they were met by Troop "F" car.

9. On Tuesday, December 9th, V.D. Sechler of Oak Grove Lodge was brought in to view Nediovitch's body and he made a positive identification of him as the man with Newman at Oak Grove Lodge on the early morning of November 27, 1941. Later this day a message was received from General Headquarters advising that bullets fired from Nedimovitch's gun were positive in comparison with fatal bullets from Newman's body.

10. The 39 Packard Coupe was identified by motor number as the one stolen in Little Rock. Finger and palm prints of Nedimovitch were forwarded to Little Rock, Arkansas Police. We have information from Arkansas that his picture has been identified by a station attendant at Little Rock where this Packard was filled with gas and oil shortly after the murder. All circumstantial evidence indicates that he is the slayer wanted at Little Rock.

11. License #770-417 on this car at the time, were reported by the owner as stolen from his car Saturday, December 6th, night,

and will be returned to the owner. The car has been released to the Adjustment Company of Springfield, Mr. King.

O.L. Viets, 1st Sgt.

#56

CC: GHQ

CC: Troop "F"

CC: File D-3099

STATEMENT OF MARGIE SMITH

THIS STATEMENT WAS MADE to Greene County Sheriff Ruel Wommack and County Attorney Bill Collinson several hours after the shooting. It was printed in the December 8, 1941 morning edition of the Springfield Daily News and is reprinted here exactly as it appeared.

My name is Margie Fae Smith. I am 19 years of age, single and lived at Walnut Grove, Missouri, until April 10, 1941, when I moved in the upstairs part of the Coffee Pot Tavern south of Galloway, Mo. I started working there for Sam Baker and continued working there after Mr. Baker sold the place to Uba Coble. I first met Milan J. Nedimovich at Amy's Grill on south Jefferson Street, Springfield, Missouri during the last part of September or first part of October, this year. At that time he was wearing a soldier's uniform and said that he was from Fort Leonard Wood.

At that time he had and was driving a Buick 8 Coach, 1937 model I believe. During the first week or ten days of October, I was with him nearly every evening. He told me that he was on furlough from Fort Leonard Wood during this time. After that I did not see him for about a month. Then one Saturday night I saw him again and he told me that he had had a wreck with the Buick, that it was in a repair shop at the fort, I believe.

TOLD OF SELLING CAR

Along about the middle of November, I saw him again on a weekend and he told me that he had sold the Buick, that he had been transferred to Arkansas and that he would have to catch a bus to Little Rock. The next time I saw him was on Sunday, November 23, 1941, or really it was in the middle of Sunday night or closer to Monday morning. He was at that time traveling on a motorcycle, which he said that he had borrowed from a soldier at Camp Robinson.

He said he had ridden all night to get up here. His little finger on the right hand was bound up and he said that he had injured it in falling off the motorcycle. I was with him on the afternoon of November 24th from 1:00 p. m. until about 5:30 p. m. I was supposed to have a date with him the evening of the 24th, but he failed to show up any more that evening. On the 25th of November, Tuesday, he and I had agreed that he would come back to the Coffee Pot about 10:00 a. m.

RODE ON MOTORCYCLE

This was to be my day off. He did not show up that morning and I caught the one o'clock bus and came to Springfield, shopped a little, went to the show and as I was ready to leave on the bus back to Galloway at 5:30 p. m., he and Velma Jones came into the Union Bus Station. They were riding on the motorcycle. All three of us rode the cycle out to the Coffee Pot, where I changed clothes. The three of us came back to town, about 7:30, then went out to Gilmore's on Kearney street and then to the Oasis on East 66 Highway. We didn't get out at the Oasis, but went on around to the flying A Terminal on Highway 66 By-pass, then back to Gilmore's, then took Velma Jones home on North Prospect, and then Jimmy and I went out to the Coffee Pot, arriving there a little after midnight. Jimmy stayed there with me until 1:30 p. m., said he had to be back in Little Rock to answer roll call the next morning. He left me and went south on the highway.

The next time I saw him was about nine-thirty p. m. Saturday night, November 29th, 1941, when he came into the Coffee Pot. He was in civilian clothes. He had on a green cloth jacket, dark wool pants and a tan shirt and no hat. He said that he had ridden the bus up from Little Rock. He also said that he had some baggage at the Union bus Terminal. After going around to a few taverns with another couple in their car, (They were Mr. and Mrs. Fred Young from down around Ozark), we let Jimmy out at the front door of the Met Hotel on College Street.

WENT TO GET ROOM

He had said that he was going to get a room for the night and he walked into the lobby. The next time I saw him was about ten p. m. Sunday night, November 30th, when he stopped by the Coffee Pot and said he had to go back to Little Rock and that he had caught a ride, and that a car was waiting for him out on the highway. He did get in a car and go on south. I do not believe that he drove because he entered the right side of the car. He had on his uniform at this time.

The next time I saw him was about 5:00 p. m. Monday evening, December 1st. He said he had been sitting in the Coffee Pot for about an hour waiting for me. He told me that he slept all day Sunday. He told me that he had gone on back to Little Rock Sunday night, that he had worked about a half hour Monday morning, when his sergeant brought him his release papers, and that his sergeant had driven him from Little Rock to Springfield Monday. He had a black grain leather bag with him. I had to work that night, so he stayed upstairs at the Coffee Pot until around 11:00 p. m. He told me he was going to hitch-hike back to Little Rock and left the Coffee Pot going south on foot. He said before he left that he would be back about Friday, December 5th.

Mr. and Mrs. Coble know that Jimmy was back at the Coffee Pot around 2:30 or 3:00 p. m. Tuesday, December 2nd.

I did not see Jimmy anymore that day or anytime until Saturday, December 6th, about 10:30 p. m., when he drove in the Coffee Pot drive in a Packard coupe alone. He had told me before he left that he was going to get a Buick in Little Rock since he could buy a car cheaper down there.

On Saturday night, November 29th, while we were at the Oasis, Jimmy gave me a diamond engagement ring and later that night gave me a wedding ring, which he told me to put in my pocket book. The box they came in was a Sass Jewelry company box.

When Jimmy left me on the morning of November 26th, 1941, about 1:30 a. m., he was dressed in his soldier's uniform. The address at which I used to write Jimmy was: Companies H &S, 43rd Engineers Regiment, Medical Detachment, Camp Robinson, Little Rock, Arkansas.

On Saturday night, December 6th, 1941, at about 11:45 P. m. Jimmy and I left the Coffee Pot in the Packard, went to Gilmore's and the Oasis and got back out to the Coffee Pot about 3:30 Sunday morning, December 7th, we went up stairs over the Coffee Pot, where Lela Nix who also works there was asleep in the double-bed where I ordinarily sleep. Jimmy said that he would go back to town and get a room, but we decided to fix him a bed on the studio couch. He slept there last night and Lela and I slept in the bed. I awoke this morning about ten-thirty. Lela had already gotten up and gone down stairs. Jimmy was still asleep and I did not awaken him, but went down and ate breakfast and came back up to the room and woke him up. This was about 11:15 this morning. We sat there and talked for a few minutes and just before noon a car drove in the driveway. Jimmy walked over to the northeast window and looked out. He then walked over to the door at the southwest part of the room. About that time I heard some one coming up the steps to the door where he was standing. Whoever it was running up the steps. Then, Jimmy had a gun in his hand. I don't know where he got it, but he must have had it on his person. I believe he fired the first shot through the glass pane in the door. Just at that time the door opened inward and a state patrolman fell forward on his face through the door.

I later learned that this patrolman was Vic Dosing. Just about that time Jimmy aimed the pistol down the steps and fired again. I could hear someone coming up the steps, but could not see who it was. When the first shot was fired I was standing in the middle of the room, and ran over to the northwest corner behind a small coat closet. When the second shot was fired, I raised up and looked out the window next to that clothes closet. After I looked out the window, I looked back at him and I'm almost positive that he had both his own gun and the gun of the fallen patrolman in his hands. At this time the door leading down the steps was partially open and Jimmy was standing with his back to the wall or facing north, partly behind the door. I screamed, "Jimmy," and he yelled, "Shut up," and pointed the small gun at me and snapped it. It didn't go off, and he threw it to the floor. I tried to crowd down behind an ironing board, and when I looked at him again, he was falling to the floor. I did not know at that time that he had been shot in the head. He writhed on the floor and lay still. I stayed behind the ironing board for what seemed several minutes and screamed for someone to come up there. When no one came I got up and walked over toward the door and saw the little gun and the big one lying on the floor within a foot of each other. Jimmy was lying on his left side with his head close to the south wall. The patrolman was lying with his head pointed east and his feet were sticking out over the door-sill. I walked over toward the door stepped over the patrolman's body, pushed open the screen and went down stairs.

I have read this four-page statement after have made same of my own free will and accord, without threat or promise of any kind having been made to me, and it is true, and I am making same to help the officers clear up the shooting at the Coffee Pot Tavern today.

MARJIE FAE SMITH

DOSING CORONER'S INQUEST TRANSCRIPT

STATE OF MISSOURI
County of Greene,

AN INQUEST, held before G. H. Boehm, Acting Coroner, Greene County, Missouri, on the 8th day of December, A.D. 1941, at 2:00 P.M. over the dead bodies of VICTOR DOSING and MILAN J. NEDIMOVICH.

Witnesses: Page:

John Love
Justice F. A. Stubbs
Miss Margie Smith
Earl Barkley
Ruel N. Wommack
O. L. Viets
U. R. Coble
Mrs. Lela Nix

AT AN INQUEST, held before the undersigned, G. H. Boehm, Acting Coroner, South Campbell Township, Greene County, Missouri, at his office, No. 227 East Olive Street, in the city of Springfield, Greene County, Missouri, at 2:00 P. M. on the 8th day of December, A.D. 1941, over the dead body of VICTOR DOSING and the dead body of MILAN J. NEDIMOVICH.

APPEARANCES

MR. E. ANDREW CARR, Assistant Prosecuting Attorney, Greene County.

A jury of six men having been duly summoned to appear at the office of he Acting Coroner, F. H. Boehm, No. 227 East Olive Street, Springfield, Missouri, and having viewed the dead bodies of the said Victor Dosing and of the said Milan J. Nedimovich, were by the Acting Coroner, in the presence of said bodies, duly sworn to diligently inquire and true presentment make in what manner and by whom deceased came to their deaths.

And thereafter, on this 8th day of December, 1941, at 2;00 P.M., the said jury of six men appeared at the office of the Acting Coroner, G. H. Boehm, 227 Olive Street, Springfield, Missouri, and having been duly sworn as to their duty, the following proceedings were had:

THE CORONER: Would it be better, Mr. Carr to take them up together or one at a time?

MR. CARR: You can hear them together to same time, but whatever you say.

THE CORONER: You understand, gentlemen, there are two dead bodies here that were killed in   the same skirmish, and we can use the same jury and handle the issues in the cases together, I think.

MR. CARR: I would like to explain to the jury just where this happened before we start. The scene of this occurrence was the Coffee Pot. Most of you are familiar with that building and know it is an unusual structure, round in the shape of a coffee pot, smaller at the top than at the bottom, out here south near Galloway, and an outside stairway leading upstairs to a room above, which is a bedroom and sleeping room. It is about, I would say, twenty-five in circumference upstairs, maybe thirty feet, with only one way to get in and out and that is the outside stairway, with the door on the west side.

****

MR. JOHN LOVE, being produced, sworn and examined, testified as follows:

EXAMINATION BY MR. CARR:

Q- State your name, please?

A- John Love.

Q- You are constable of what township?

A- Deputy constable of Clay Township.

Q- Deputy constable of Clay Township?

A- That is right.

Q- Did you either on last Saturday or Sunday see Milan J. Nedimovich?

A- Yes.

Q- Where did you see him the first time?

A- Coming down the steps. The first distinct view I got of him was his legs coming down the steps after Graham and Dosing were shot.

Q- Did you see him any time Saturday?

A- No.

Q- Did you go down to the Coffee Pot to check on his whereabouts on Sunday?

A- I did, yes, sir.

Q- What time did you go down?

A- It was between twelve and one o'clock.

Q- State what you did when you went down there.

A- I went in and asked Mr. Coble, the man that runs the place, if Nedimovich was upstairs, and he said, "Yes". Then I went back down to Jones Filling Station and told Jones to call the patrol, and then this son-in-law of this man who was shot in Arkansas and myself got in my car and drove up right south of the Coffee Pot and parked on the east side of the road headed north.

Q- That is across the highway?

A- Across the highway, a little bit south.

Q- Did you wait there for some time?

A- I waited there until the patrol came, but in the meantime Mr. Stubbs, the justice down there, came by us and turned around and parked his car behind us, got out and got in the car with this Standke and me and we waited there until the state patrol came.

Q- What was your purpose in going up there for this Nedimovich?

A- Well, shall I start at the beginning and tell how come me to be down there?

Q- Were you there after any particular car?

A- I was up there checking on him on the Packard that was parked in back of the Coffee Pot, back of the building.

Q- What was it that lead you to call the highway patrol?

A- I was at home and Judge Stubbs called me and asked if I remembered this soldier's name that had stolen the Buick down thee on the 9th of October. I didn't because it is an unusual name. I knew it started with an "N" and ended with "vich", but I didn't remember all of it. So I told him I could call the highway patrol office and get it because they had the record, because I called it once or twice before in dealing with the insurance company on the Buick in the fall. He told me for me to come on down because he wanted to talk to me. When I got down to his office Mr. Jones and this Standke man, the son-in-law of the man who was killed, were there.

Q- That is the son-in-law of the man who was killed in Arkansas?

A- That is right. He asked me to call the state patrol and I called them. I don't remember who it was I talked to, but anyway they gave me his name. I told them we thought he was in the neighborhood somewhere so they told me to go on back down – They first said Smith's filling station. I told them I didn't know any filling stations down there by that name. Then they said it was Jones station. So we got into the car, that is Jones and Standke got in Jones' truck and I followed them, and Judge Stubbs went on about his other duties is how come him not to go with us. When we got down to Jones filling station, Jones came out and told me he had saw the Packard parked in back of the Coffee Pot and he was confident it was the one at his place Saturday night. When we arrested this fellow October 9th with this stolen Buick he had been hanging around Jones filling station before we got him and Jones remembered him and when he drove in there Saturday night and traded the tire and wheel off this Packard for gas, Jones remembered him, recognized him. I went back up there and went in and asked the man that ran the place – I believe his name is Coble – if this fellow was there. He told me yes, he was upstairs. I asked him if his name was Nedimovich. He said yes, he was upstairs. I asked if that was his Packard and he said yes. He had the license number and description of the car already written down and told me he was getting ready to go out and call the patrol because he got suspicious. He had read the account of it in the morning paper.

Q- That was what Coble told you?
A- Yes, sir.

Q- That is the man that ran the Coffee Pot?
A- Yes. So I ordered a coke, threw them a dime down on the counter and left it sitting there and told him I would be back in a few minutes and went down and told Jones to call the patrol.

Q- Where he was waiting across the highway?
A- He was across the highway in a position where he could watch the steps.

Q- You did learn from Coble that this fellow was there?
A- He was upstairs. And then when the patrol blew in before I could get across the highway they had got out of the car and were inside. They had already stepped in and were talking. I don't know what they said to Mr. Coble. They had said whatever they had to say to him and was going through the

kitchen and I believe Mr. Dosing had the back kitchen door open and was going down some steps. I hollered three times to wait a minute. I don't know whether he didn't hear me, didn't recognize me or what.

Q- Dosing and Graham went out the back door of the kitchen?
A- Yes, sir.

Q- The steps start at the back door?
A- No, you have to go around the curve of the building, go up the south side of the building.

Q- That is an open stairway?
A- That is an open stairway and has got banisters on the south side.

Q- What happened?
A- Mr. Dosing went up and opened the door, pushed it about half way open, I judge. The door started to open and I saw this arm come out the door and saw the powder from the shot and Mr. Dosing started to fall and just then two reports almost together. One of them went off, you could see the smoke go up in the door and the other one in my opinion is the shot that hit Mr. Graham. And then another shot, as best I remember that went off right after that, and as he hit Graham, Graham fell forward to one side against the banister. I shot at him. He shot at me twice and I shot the second time at him. Graham lost his balance and stumbled against me. We went backward sideways down the steps.

Q- You are sure the door was open when the first shot was fired?

A- I am positive of it. I was standing where I could see his gun when the door opened and I saw it go off.

Q- You know the first shot did not come through the glass?
A- I am sure it did not come through the glass.

Q- Did Dosing ever fire his pistol?
A- There was two shots went off together, almost together and one the smoke boiled up in the door.

Q- Two separate portion of smoke there in the doorway?
A- I saw the smoke from the soldier's gun and saw the smoke from the second shot that went off boil up in the door.

Q- You don't know whether the second shot was from the inside?
A- No, it was not from the gun inside. It was from the door. And Graham shot then. I think his shot is the one that hit the outside of the building because he had throwed himself over against the banister and when he shot the second time, just as the gun went off before I could shoot again, Mr. Graham staggered against me. We went down the steps, I don't know just how. I remember throwing out my arm to catch him. I was off balance myself. I was standing with one foot up, the left foot on the high step and the right foot on the lower step.

Q- Did you both go down he steps?
A- Both went down the steps. I said, "He got him, didn't he"? He said, "Yes, he got my buddy". We got inside the kitchen.

Q- Through the back door of the kitchen?

A- Through the back door of the kitchen and Graham had got in the counter part, where the counter is in the front room and I was standing in the door when I heard this man start down the steps. I ran to the south window but didn't get there in time. I saw him go down and just as he started to turn the corner I shot slant ways south to west through the window and he turned and ran back up the stairs and I shot at his legs again through the south window as he went up the stairs and my old gun jammed.

Q- The south window is level with the steps?

A- A little bit above the bottom of the steps. The top of it is about on the level with the banister that goes up. When I was standing there trying to get my gun to work again I heard a gun go off on the outside. That was the last shot that was fired.

Q- Do you know where that gun was fired?

A- It sounded to me like it came from the outside of the building. I wouldn't swear to that for sure, but I know it wasn't upstairs and it wasn't there inside.

Q- Do you know when the door glass was broken?

A- No, I don't know that. It was probably broken by me or by Dosing's shot as he went down.

Q- What happened after this last shot that you heard?

A- This girl started screaming and somebody started down the steps. In the meantime I was working with my old gun and got it so it would work again. I ran back to the south window and took a rest – I was holding it right directly on whoever would have to come down the steps and when I started to pull the trigger I saw a girl. I ran to the kitchen door and Mr. Coble, me and him together, pulled her in.

Q- To the back kitchen door?

A- The back door. She either fainted or fell. Anyway she was laying flat on the bottom step right in front of the back door.

Q- How long a time had elapsed between the time you heard the last shot and the time you saw her coming down the steps?

A- She probably screamed up there a couple or three minutes; hard to judge a thing like that.

Q- As far as you know this door up at the top of the steps had never been closed after Dosing fell through?

A- No, it was still open part way; at least, after I walked outside, after the rest of the boys come from town. In the meantime after we got inside after the last shot was fired, Mr. Graham said, "Is there anybody that will go for help?" I said, "Stubbs is supposed to be on the outside. Holler for him." He opened the door and hollered and ran up the highway toward Jones' filling station. Then Mr. Graham got up and started out, got to his car and went off. The people asked me to stay. I stayed at the window and watched. I was standing kind of back from the stairway, back up in the backyard a ways.

Q- Graham went out the front door and got in his car?

A- And drove off.

Q- Where did he go, which way?

A- I don't know. I was watching the window.

Q- Who did go upstairs after the girl came down?

A- It was one of the troopers, and I think Judge Stubbs was either second or third going up the steps.

Q- You didn't see this Nedimovich get hit or fall?
A- No, because where I was I couldn't see him.

Q- What kind of gun did you shoot?
A- A thirty- two.

Q- Do you have it with you?
A- Yes.

Q- You fired two shots?
A- On the steps and two through the windows.

Q- You fired four shots in all?
A- I fired four shots. There were two left and the patrol fired them.

Q- Was your gun fully loaded?
A- It had four shells in it, and when I finally got the gun broke – I couldn't break it at first, I finally got it broke and I tried to skip the spent shells up that slipped between the ejector and under the chamber and I had quite a time getting them loose. When I finally got them out I put this other two shells in my pocket. That is when I heard the girl coming down the steps I only had two shells in the gun.

Q- Where was Mr. Stubbs at the time the troopers were going up the stairway?
A- When I left him in the front he was in the car, him and Mr. Standke got out and they were standing, so I understand,

right south of the building, right in line with the landing of the steps in the top going in the door.

Q- Did you see him out there, or do you know that from what you heard?

A- I wouldn't say for sure I saw him when I was going up the stair. I saw them out of the car in the yard there.

Q- South of the building?

A- I wouldn't place them exactly where they said they were, but I did see them in that general direction. Things happened so fast we didn't have time to locate anybody.

Q- Do you know who was upstairs when the troopers went up there?

A- This girl and him that is all I saw.

Q- By this girl you mean Margie Smith?

A- That is right.

Q- About what time did the shooting take place? Pretty close to noon?

A- No, it was after noon. I would say around one, or maybe ten or fifteen minutes after. Anyway it was perhaps two or three minutes of twelve when he called me to come down there to his office.

Q- Do you know what kind of gun Mr. Stubbs was using?

A- He has a Colts, I believe a thirty- eight. I never brought the gun. He requested when he turned it over to me not to disfigure it in any way. The man, when I was talking about it down at Jones filling station, said it was a thirty- eight.

Q- Do you know whether it was his gun?

A- He said he was once in the secret service; went in from 1914 to 1919, five years.

Q- Did you finally go upstairs?

A- I did, yes, after Stubbs and this patrolman went up. I was up there all together three times, I think, before they took the bodies out. I went in and was talking to this girl when Mr. Kinser came up and requested I let him in. I opened the door and told this girl she would have to go with him and she said she wouldn't go without her coat. I told Mr. Kinser I would go and get her coat for her. That was the third time I was up there. I went up. There were some officers in the room. I asked someone inside for the coat and they said she wouldn't need it right then; they were not going to take her up until after the bodies were removed.

Q- Did you go up there after the other patrolmen and the sheriff and Stubbs went up?

A- I think I went up there before the sheriff got there. In fact, I don't think I saw the sheriff until at least thirty minutes after the other boys got there.

Q- Did you have any conservation with the girl when she first came down?

A- I did.

Q- What was said?

A- She came in there screaming and berating them because they had killed him. I told her to shut up and she said, "You killed him when you shot through the window". I said I couldn't because I shot at his legs. Then she said, "Yes, you shot through both legs". Then she finally said the shot that killed him came from the outside.

Q- This all took place before you went out of the kitchen the second time?

A- Yes, we were in the front room when the conversation took place. That is the way she told it to me now. She first said they had killed him and I asked her who killed him. She said, "You did". I said, "I hope so". Then she said that I shot him when he passed the window. I told her I couldn't because I was shooting at his legs; that was all I could see, was his legs.

Q- When Mr. Coble told you he thought he was involved in this Arkansas matter, did he say anything else about him?

A- If I remember right, they said they didn't have any suspicion of him until they read this article.

Q- You mean the account of the Little Rock murder?

A- Yes. The paper was lying on the counter and he had the license number and general description of the car right on that, both pieces of paper.

Q- Mr. Coble did?

A- Yes, sir.

Q- Was the car there at the time?

A- The car was in the back, parked right west of the Coffee shop.

Q- When you did go upstairs Vic Dosing was already dead, was he?

A- Oh, yes, in my opinion he was dead before he ever touched the floor.

Q- And, Nedimovich was dead at that time?

A- Yes.

Q- How long after the last shot was fired before you all went upstairs?

A- I would say ten or fifteen minutes.

Q- Where was Graham in the meantime?

A- I don't know. I don't know where he went to because I was watching the window. All I saw was him starting toward his car. I had watched him until I saw he made it in the car and then I went back to watching the window.

Q- When did this murder take place in Arkansas?

A- I don't know, to be honest with you, because I don't take the paper and as a general rule I don't look at a paper over two or three times a week. In fact, I had not heard of the case, had not read anything until Mr. Jones and this son-in-law were talking about it.

Q- How did the son-in-law happen to be in that vicinity?

A- He lives he told me, in Kansas City and was on the way to his father-in-law's funeral and just by accident stopped at Jones filling station and got to talking about the murder. That is how come them to be at Stubb's office. I don't know what Jones told him, but he described this Packard he had in there the night before he traded the tire and wheel for this gas. He recognized him because he had been hanging around there before we arrested him on the 9th of October.

Q- Do you know whether Standke had a gun with him?

A- Yes, he had a gun.

Q- Did he have it with him at the time of the shooting?

A- He had it with him. Stuck it out of the –

Q- I mean the son-in-law, Standke?

A- Yes, he had. He showed it to me down at Jones filling station.

Q- Did he have it on his person when he and Stubbs were down there?

A- He had it in his car. He went over to his car and got it and come over and put in my car.

Q- Did Mr. Stubbs have another gun beside the one Standke had?

A- No, he has no gun at all. This is his gun I have.

Q- Was he using Standke's gun during the shooting?

A- The judge?

Q- Judge Stubbs?

A- He had it before I ever left the car.

Q- Standke didn't have any gun?

A- No, none at all.

BY THE CORONER:

Q- John, where did you shoot? You said you shot four times – down below or way up on top?

A- Twice on the stairway.

Q- Were you way up on top when you shot?

A- I was about three steps from the top, not over four.

Q- Was that hole in the transom, in the window, do you know how that happened?

A- No, I don't, I don't know which one. I was positive of this fact: Dosing did push the door open and I heard someone shoot him from the inside of the room. His hand and arm came up. The barrel looked to me to be about that long (indicating) I would judge it to be a thirty-eight, from the size of it, a small thirty-eight.

Q- Could you tell the jury whether Dosing had his gun drawn when he opened the door?

A- Dosing had his gun drawn and Graham drew his, either, when he came up the steps or at the top and I also had my hand in my overcoat pocket. I had my hand on it when I started up the steps.

Q- You know both officers had their guns open?

A- Yes, when they went through the place Dosing had his gun in his right hand. When he pushed the door open, I won't say for sure Dosing's gun went off twice only by this fact, the smoke boiled up in the stairway.

Q- Two different times?

A- The first shot, the shot that killed Dosing, he stuck his gun out and the barrel of the gun was outside the door casing when it went off right in Dosing's face.

Q- Do you know which hand he had the gun in?

A- Had it in his right hand because it came out by the north side of the door.

Q- That door opens into the stairway running down to the west?

A- Yes, sir.

Q- The door opens from the right back to the left?
A- Yes, sir.

Q- A glass paneled door?
A- Glass panel, opening in.

Q- Where you saw the gun come out as it over on the north side?
A- On the north side of the door facing.

BY THE CORONER:
    Q- You saw Dosing shot did you, right there by this man?
    A- Yes, I saw Dosing shot. I saw the gun in the hand that held it and saw the smoke from the gun and saw Dosing fall.

    Q- But you are not sure whether he shot again?
    A- When his gun went off the smoke boiled up in the door. He was falling and I was behind Graham.

    Q- At the time you saw the smoke boil up there were two shots there together?
    A- Yes, sir.

    Q- Were there more shots after that from upstairs?
    A- Yes, from the inside. He never did come out until after we got down the steps and he run down.

WITNESS EXCUSED

****

JUSTICE f. A. Stubbbs, being produced, sworn and examined, testified as follows:

EXAMINATION BY MR. CARR:

Q- You are Judge Stubbs?

A- Yes.

Q- Justice of the peace?

A- Yes.

Q- Living at Galloway?

A- Yes, sir.

Q- Were you present in the car that you have heard Mr. Love describe parked across the Highway, from the Coffee Pot?

A- I am.

Q- On Sunday morning?

A- Sunday about twelve in the morning.

Q- Who else was in the car with you beside Mr. Love?

A- Another man, the son-in-law of the man killed in Arkansas. I don't know his name.

Q- Standke?

A- Something like that.

Q- Did John Love get out of the car first?

A- What do you mean?

Q- To go across? You all were seated there waiting for the patrol to come out?

A- We drove across, drove right up to the Coffee Pot.

Q- Had the patrol got there when you drove across?

A- It got there about the same time. John said, "There they come." He already had his engine running. We shot across the highway right up to the south side of the Coffee Pot. John got out and went to the patrol and me and Grant sat in the car.

Q- You and Grant?

A- Whatever his name is.

Q- You and Standke sat in the car Love was driving. Where were Graham and Dosing?

A- I couldn't see where they were at, too far west. I don't know where they were. The next time I seen them they were coming from the north.

Q- You were parked on the side of the stairway looking up?

A- Yes, sir.

Q- Who went up the stairway?

A- Dosing and another patrol. I didn't know him, and John.

Q- Were they all three together?

A- No, Dosing was in front. John and this other patrol just went side by side.

Q- State what you saw took place?

A- I jumped out of the car and this man lent me his gun. I didn't have any gun.

Q- What kind of gun was it?

A- I don't know. Must have been a thirty- eight, something like that. I didn't examine it. All I said was, "Can I depend on it"? He said, "You sure can". I jumped out and ran right down to the stairway. I seen this fellow open the door and when he opened the door, about the time Dosing got there, he reached out, I don't know whether he ever got hold of the knob or not, if he didn't he was awful close to it, and about the time the door opened the shot was fired. The gun come on the outside. I could see the gun.

Q- Did it come through the glass?
A- No, the door opened.

Q- Whatever hand fired this gun?
A- It was on the right hand. He was on the north side of the door facing and where I stood I could see him, but I couldn't see this other boy.

Q- You were standing about even with the foot of the stairs, just south of the foot of the stairs?
A- No, about half way between the stairs, just about fifteen foot from the foundation of the building is where I was.

Q- When the door opened back this way, you could see in?
A- Looking up you could see them up there on the inside, see their heads.

Q- Whose heads?
A- That boy and this girl.

Q- Did you see her through the door?
A- I could see her running around in there, yes.

Q- This first shot that was fired by that hand sticking out with the gun, you know that was Nedimovich?

A- I know it was the man on the inside.

Q- That was the man you later found upstairs that fired?

A- Yes.

Q- Dosing fell forward, did he?

A- Fell forward and as he fell he shot.

Q- You are sure he shot as he fell?

A- Yes, sir.

Q- Do you know whether anyone was struck by that bullet?

A- No, I sure don't. What was done was done in a minute's time, I guess.

Q- Now when was the next shot fired?

A- This other patrol he fired two shots.

Q- That was Mr. Graham?

A- Whatever his name was, I don't know. He was the one that was with Dosing. And this other fellow at the door, I seen him grab this other fellow and he fell kind of over against the banister like and John jerked out his gun, he already had, and he shot, and in a second they just kind of backed down the steps. I guess they were a couple or three steps up. When they come around that corner there was another shot fired. I don't know whether John fired it or whether he did. I don't know which one fired. I thought John was hit.

Q- Did you see Nedimovich come out of the door and come down the steps?

A- I did.

Q- Where did he go?

A- He was running around north. I raised my gun to shoot but I couldn't shoot because I knowed there was people in the kitchen and it was just small weatherboard on the side. I stood right there until he got up the flight of steps where Dosing was laying and he drew his gun after he had spotted me and I leveled down on him.

Q- He was outside of the door?

A- He was outside the door, completely out.

Q- The door had never been shut?

A- No, it couldn't be shut. Dosing was caught in the door.

Q- You shot at him, did you?

A- Yes, sir.

Q- What did he do?

A- He drawed back his hand and went in the door. That is all I know. The next thing this girl jumped out the door. I drawed the gun for him. She fell on the banister, which are on the side. I stood there a minute and this fellow jumped out of the car and come to me and put his hand on the door and said, "You done the work".

Q- That is Standke came over to you?

A- Yes.

Q- You say the girl came out to you?

A- Yes, just as he went in she come out. It wasn't but just a flash. That is all there is to it.

Q- Where did she go?

A- I don't know. She come down the steps. I was watching the others.

Q- Were there any more shots fired?

A- Not that I ever heard.

Q- Did you see where Graham went? Did you see him come down the steps?

A- Graham?

Q- That is the second patrolman on the steps?

A- Yes, him and John they had their arms around each other. They went around north. I was left there.

Q- You aimed this gun at him and fired when he was outside on the stairway?

A- Yes.

Q- Do you think you hit him?

A- I tried to.

Q- Did he fall?

A- He just fell in the door. That is all I know. I never did see a glimpse of him anywhere there. I don't know what patrol it was or where he come from. He went up with the Trooper.

Q- There never was a shot fired until after that?

A- I never heard any.

Q- When he come running down the steps was there any blood on Nedimovich?

A- Now you are asking a question.

Q- None that you saw?

A- No.

Q- What did you do after you fired that shot?

A- I stood there and this fellow come to me and I said, "I believe I will go to Dosing". He said, "That fellow will kill you". I said, "If I got him, he won't".

Q- Did you go upstairs?

A- No, not then. Someone from the inside or somewhere there hollered, "Go and call for more help. We need it." I told that fellow there, "You got behind that car and stay there". I said, "I will run to the telephone and call the highway patrol", and I did. I don't know who I talked to. I told them what had happened and one patrol was killed and another was shot and I believed another man. And at the time I got back there, it seemed as though these patrol that was there don't belong there. They had taken a call of what was going on out here and run upstairs with his rifle and I followed him.

Q- And as far as you know, you were the first people to go up there after the shooting stopped?

A- Yes.

Q- What did you find when you got up there?

A- Dosing was laying there in the floor dead.

Q- He was laying right where you saw him fall?

A- No, back – He crawled probably a foot or more, and his elbow was through the door. This other fellow was laying with his head south and his feet at Dosing's head.

Q- Where was his gun?

A- His gun was behind him, laying on his left side and his gun behind him and it cocked. I don't know just exactly where Dosing's gun was. I couldn't tell you.

Q- Was it on the floor?

A- It was.

Q- It wasn't in his holster?

A- No.

Q- The two bodies were laying within two feet of each other?

A- His feet were laying within six inches of Dosing's head, I judge.

Q- Did you examine his gun?

A- I never touched the guns.

Q- You didn't examine either one?

A- No sir, never did.

Q- You don't know how many shots were fired by him?

A- No, I don't know because the patrol began to come in and I figured it wasn't my place to do that. I don't know how many times there had been shots or nothing about it. I know I just shot one time.

Q- You saw Nedimovich shoot Dosing, did you?

A- Whatever his name was.

Q- The fellow that was lying dead upstairs?

A- I seen him shoot him and seen him shoot this other fellow.

Q- You saw him shoot Graham?

A- Yes.

Q- You don't know whether your shot hit Nedimovich or not when he was outside the

stairway?

A- No, a man couldn't say that, you know.

BY THE CORONER:

Q- Where were you shooting from? Just where were you?

A- I was in about fifteen foot of the steps.

Q- Down below?

A- Yes, beside the steps and he was just right straight, you might say, up there.

Q- But you saw this man shoot Vic Dosing?

A- I sure did.

Q- Now when was the next shot fired?

A- This other patrol he fired two shots.

Q- That was Mr. Graham?

A- Whatever his name was, I don't know. He was the one that was with Dosing. And this other fellow at the door, I seen him grab this other fellow and he fell kind of over against the banister like and John jerked out his gun, he already had, and he shot, and in a second they just kind of backed down them steps. I guess they were a couple or three steps up. When they come around that corner there was another shot fired. I don't know whether John fired it or whether he did. I don't know which one fired. I thought John was hit.

Q- Did you see Nedimovich come out of the door and come down the steps?

A- I did.

Q- Where did he go?

A- He was running around north. I raised my gun to shoot but I couldn't shoot because I knowed there was people in the kitchen and it was just small weatherboard on the side. I stood right there until he got up the flight of steps where Dosing was laying and he drawed his gun after he had spotted me and I leveled down on him.

Q- He was outside of the door?

A- He was outside the door, completely out.

Q- The door had never been shut?

A- No, it couldn't be shut. Dosing was caught in the door.

Q- You shot at him, did you?

A- Yes, sir.

Q- What did he do?

A- He drawed back his hand and went in the door. That is all I know. The next thing this girl jumped out the door. I drawed the gun for him. She fell on the banister which are on the side. I stood there a minute and this fellow jumped out of the car and come to me and put his hand on the door and said, "You done the work".

Q- That is Standke came over to you?

A- Yes.

Q- You say the girl came out to you?

A- Yes, just as he went in she come out. It wasn't but just a flash. That is all there is to it.

Q- Where did she go?

A- I don't know. She come down the steps. I was watching the others.

Q- Were there any more shots fired?

A- Not that I ever heard.

Q- Did you see where Graham went? Did you see him come down the steps?

A- Graham?

Q- That is the second patrolman on the steps?

A- Yes, him and John they had their armsa round each other. They went around north. I was left there.

Q- You aimed this gun at him and fired when he was outside on the stairway?

A- Yes.

Q- Do you think you hit him?

A- I tried to.

Q- Did he fall?

A- He just fell in the door. That is all I know. I never did see a glimpse of him anywhere there. I don't know what patrol it was or where he come from. He went up with the Trooper.

Q- There never was a shot fired until after that?

A- I never heard any.

Q- When he come running down the steps was there any blood on Nedimovich?

A- Now you are asking a question.

Q- None that you saw?

A- No.

Q- What did you do after you fired that shot?

A- I stood there and this fellow come to me and I said, "I believe I will go to Dosing". He said, "That fellow will kill you". I said, "If I got him, he won't".

Q- Did you go upstairs?

A- No, not then. Someone from the inside or somewhere there hollered, "Go and call for more help. We need it." I told that fellow there, "You got behind that car and stay there". I said, "I will run to the telephone and call the highway patrol", and I did. I don't know who I talked to. I told them what had happened and one patrol was killed and another was shot and I believed another man. And at the time I got back there, it seemed as though these patrol that was there don't belong there. They had taken a call of what was going on out here and run upstairs with his rifle and I followed him.

Q- And as far as you know, you were the first people to go up there after the shooting stopped?

A- Yes.

Q- What did you find when you got up there?

A- Dosing was laying there in the floor dead.

Q- He was laying right where you saw him fall?

A- No, back – He crawled probably a foot or more, and his elbow was through the door. This other fellow was laying with his head south and his feet at Dosing's head.

Q- Where was his gun?

A- His gun was behind him, laying on his left side and his gun behind him and it cocked. I don't know just exactly where Dosing's gun was. I couldn't tell you.

Q- Was it on the floor?

A- It was.

Q- It wasn't in his holster?

A- No.

Q- The two bodies were laying within two feet of each other?

A- His feet were laying within six inches of Dosing's head, I judge.

Q- Did you examine his gun?

A- I never touched the guns.

Q- You didn't examine either one?

A- No sir, never did.

Q- You don't know how many shots were fired by him?

A- No, I don't know because the patrol began to come in and I figured it wasn't my place to do that. I don't know how many times there had been shots or nothing about it. I know I just shot one time.

Q- You saw Nedimovich shoot Dosing, did you?
A- Whatever his name was.

Q- The fellow that was lying dead upstairs?
A- I seen him shoot him and seen him shoot this other fellow.

Q- You saw him shoot Graham?
A- Yes.

Q- You don't know whether your shot hit Nedimovich or not when he was outside the stairway?
A- No, a man couldn't say that, you know.

BY THE CORONER:

Q- Where were you shooting from? Just where were you?
A- I was in about fifteen foot of the steps.

Q- Down below?
A- Yes, beside the steps and he was just right straight, you might say, up there.

Q- But you saw this man shoot Vic Dosing?
A- I sure did.

BY MR. CARR:

Q- (showing witness paper) Is this is a fair representation of the upstairs part, just where were you in relation to that stairway?

A- This the stairway?

Q- Yes.

A- He was standing astride of Dosing's feet and he just went head foremost. I don't know where his body laid, or what.

Q- Is this a fair representation of the inside there, as you saw it, a round, circular building?

A- Yes, that is the way it is.

BY THE CORONER:

Q- Do you have any idea how that hole was torn through that glass in that door?

A- My estimate is that John or this other patrol shot through the door.

Q- Mr. Graham, you mean?

A- Yes.

Q- John, who do you call "John"?

A- That is the constable out there, Mr. Love. This is my estimate, because they were shooting on the same angle of that door.

Q- And you think you surely saw this soldier boy shoot Vic Dosing after the door was opened?

A- I know I did, yes.

BY MR. CARR:

Q- You don't recall hearing the glass breaking, do you?

A- No.

BY JUROR:

Q- Which way does this door open where this stairway goes up? Was the hinges on this side on the door, the knob here, or was it on this side (indicating)?

A- I don't really understand the question.

Q- Was it opened like that door there, to the side?

A- Yes, sir.

Q- Opened just like that, and the stairway come down this way and come around?

A- Yes, sir.

BY MR. CARR:

Q- The door swung to the south?

A- The door swung to the south and he was on the north side, whatever his name was, this soldier boy. He was on the north side and I could see him from where I was at.

Q- You were on the west side of this place?

A- On the south, you might say, a little bit west, I guess. I was right where I could look through the door.

BY THE CORONER:

Q- I didn't have in mind the proper direction, but I guess the door hung like this on its hinges?

A- And the screen was the same way. It went back to the south.

WITNESS EXCUSED

****

MISS MARJIE SMITH, being produced, sworn and examined, testified as follows:

EXAMINATION BY MR. CARR:

Q- Your name is Margie Smith?

A- Yes, sir.

Q- You live, or formerly lived at Walnut Grove?

A- Yes, sir.

Q- Have you been employed for the last month or so at the Coffee Pot?

A- Yes, I was. I had been working there all summer.

Q- Been working there all summer?

A- Since the tenth of April.

Q- Since April tenth of this year?

A- Yes.

Q- Where do you live?

A- I lived upstairs at the Coffee Pot.

Q- Did anyone else live there?

A- Last summer there was some more working down there lived there, and Mrs. Nix is there every weekend nights.

Q- Mrs. Nix – you mean Lela Nix?

A- Yes, sir.

Q- Was she there over this past weekend, December 6th and 7th?
A- Yes, sir.

Q- How long had you known Milan Nedimovich – Is that the way you pronounce his name?
A- Ever since about the last of September.

Q- Did you ever know him under any other name?
A- Yes, when I first started going with him he told me his name was Donnahue, Jimmie Donnahue.

Q- Jimmie Donnahue?
A- Yes, sir.

Q- When you first met him was it here in Springfield?
A- Yes, it was.

Q- Was he in uniform then?
A- Yes, sir.

Q- Where was he stationed at that time?
A- He said he was stationed at Fort Leonard Wood.

Q- Did you see him afterward at different times from September on up to December 7th?
A- Yes, I did.

Q- Several, times a week?
A- No, there was an interval of about four weeks I didn't see him at all. That was after he told me his name was Donnahue. I

didn't see him anymore and he came and told me his name was Nedimovich.

Q- Had he been transferred anywhere?
A- Yes, he said he was being transferred to Camp Robinson, Arkansas.

Q- At little Rock?
A- Yes, sir.

Q- When did you see him last week? What day did you see him last week?
A- I saw him Saturday night and Sunday.

Q- He came up here Saturday night?
A- I saw him a week ago today.

Q- Did he come up on this Saturday night?
A- Yes, sir.

Q- What time did he get there?
A- About ten thirty, I think.

Q- What was his means of travel?
A- He was in his Packard.

Q- Coupe?
A- Yes, sir.

Q- Were you with him Saturday night?
A- Yes, I got off about a quarter after eleven. It took me about half an hour to dress, and then we came to Springfield.

Q- Where did you go here?

A- We went out to Gilmore's first and came out in about forty-five minutes and went to the Oasis; stayed a little while and came back up town.

Q- Did you go back out to the Coffee Pot?

A- Yes, we did.

Q- Did he stay out there?

A- Yes, he did.

Q- He stayed upstairs there that night?

A- Yes.

Q- Who else was there?

A- Lela Nix.

Q- That is the other lady that worked there?

A- Yes.

Q- Where did he sleep?

A- He slept on the studio couch.

Q- That is on the north side of the room?

A- The north side.

Q- There is also a double bed – Who slept there?

A- Lela Nix and I.

Q- What time did you all go back to the Coffee Pot?

A- Three o'clock, between three and three thirty.

Q- That would be Sunday morning?

A- Yes.

Q- What time did you wake up Sunday morning?

A- About ten thirty.

Q- Did you get up right away and go downstairs?

A- Yes, I got up and dressed and went down and ate breakfast.

Q- Was Lela Nix already up and gone?

A- Yes, she came back up while I was dressing and we went down together and ate breakfast.

Q- He was still there?

A- Yes, he had not gotten up yet.

Q- Did you wake him then?

A- No, I didn't wake him until I came back up.

Q- You went down, ate breakfast and came back up?

A- Yes, sir.

Q- What time was it when you came back upstairs?

A- I imagine about a quarter or ten to eleven.

Q- What happened there between that time and noon?

A- Well, Mrs. Nix came up for a few minutes. We were talking and talked about going to Florida.

Q- You and Nedimovich?

A- Yes, and I was going to pack and go down to my sisters Sunday evening and was going to stay there next week and we were supposed to leave next weekend. And he was just getting up to leave when these patrolmen came.

Q- Had he got up and dressed when you came back upstairs, or did you wake him up?

A- When he went to bed he didn't undress at all.

Q- You just woke him up?

A- I woke him up. He got up and combed his hair, and washed his face. That is all he did.

Q- Did Mrs. Nix go downstairs?

A- Yes. Yes, she went down just before the troopers came.

Q- Did you see the troopers come?

A- No, I didn't know who was there until he shot Dosing and he fell through the door.

Q- When you first knew the troopers were there?

A- We were sitting on the studio and Jimmie stood up to leave and about that time a car drove in. He looked out the window. I didn't think about it because there was always customers driving in. He looked out the window but didn't say anything. I never thought anything about it. He didn't act suspicious and walked across to the door and stopped. He walked kind of slow. I heard them coming up the steps, making a lot of noise.

Q- Did he stand there by the door?

A- Yes, just about that far from the door (indicating).

Q- Which side of the door?

A- About the center.

Q- Looking out the glass?

A- Yes, sir.

Q- Was there a curtain over that glass?

A- Yes, sir. I said, "Jimmie, who is that? What are they making such a noise for"? I was standing in the middle of the room at that time, and about that time he shot and the trooper fell through in the door.

Q- When did he get his gun?

A- When the trooper got to the door. He didn't have the gun out until the trooper was practically at the door. I didn't see any gun. I didn't know what was taking place.

Q- But you know he did not have the gun out when the trooper first started upstairs?

A- No, he didn't.

Q- You don't know where he got the gun?

A- I think he got it from his right pocket.

Q- When you first saw the gun is when he did the shooting?

A- Yes, sir.

Q- Did he open the door or did he shoot the trooper through the glass?

A- I am sure he never walked through the door. I don't believe he opened the door.

Q- You were looking at him?

A- The trooper had opened the screen and was between the screen and the door on the top step and Jimmie was there standing about the center of the door, and I am sure he fired the gun in the trooper's face. When the trooper fell forward against the door he fell in. He didn't push it entirely open, just about half way.

Q- Do you want to state to these men he fired through the glass?

A- I am pretty sure he did.

Q- Did you hear the glass breaking?

A- Yes, sir.

BY THE CORONER:

Q- Did he shoot twice through the glass and then after the door was open shoot again?

A- He never shot after the trooper was killed. I don't think he moved a muscle. He fell right where he was.

Q- When the trooper fell in, he fell on his face?

A- Yes, sir.

Q- What did Jimmie do?

A- There was somebody else on the steps. I couldn't see who it was because by that time I was in the corner. He shot again on the steps. I don't know who it was on the steps or whether he hit him or not, but he did shoot again.

Q- Where was he standing?

A- He was standing right at the patrol's head.

Q- In the meantime you had gone over to the north side of the room?

A- Yes, there was a little cupboard there. I was over there.

Q- A make- shift clothes closet for that room?

A- Yes.

Q- What did he do after he shot the second time?

A- He turned around and snapped the gun at me and when he did I fell down behind the ironing board and when I raised up he fell. He fell on his left side.

Q- Did you hear any more shots?

A- One more shot.

Q- Could you tell whether it was on the inside of the room or the outside?

A- No.

Q- Did you ever see him reach and get Dosing's gun?

A- No. I know he had both guns in his hands.

Q- He snapped one gun at you?

A- He snapped the smaller one at me.

BY THE CORONER:

Q- Which hand did he have the smaller gun in?

A- I don't know.

Q- In which hand did he have the larger gun?

A- I couldn't tell you.

BY MR. CARR:

Q- That gun he snapped at you – What did he do with that gun?

A- Dropped it to the floor.

Q- Do you know whether he was right handed or left handed?

A- I think he was right handed.

Q- You have seen him write, haven't you?

A- I think – Yes, he was right handed.

Q- Do you know for sure?

A- I was trying to think. I was thinking when I seen him write, I am pretty sure he was right handed, yes.

Q- After he snapped the gun at you and threw the smaller one to the floor, did he still have a gun in his hand?

A- Yes, sir.

Q- Do you know whether it was Dosing's gun?

A- Yes, it was the larger gun, about that big (indicating). It was the larger gun.

Q- Did you have any knowledge that he had a gun before the troopers came out there?

A- No, I didn't. I didn't have the slightest idea. I didn't know what it was all about when they began shooting.

Q- Did he tell you anything about the Packard car, where it came from?

A- When he was here before he told me he was going to Little Rock and buy a car down there because he could get one cheaper down there. He said he was going to get a Buick before he left here, but he came back with this Packard. I asked him how he happened to get a Packard. He said he run on to this and he liked it better.

Q- Did he say anything to you from the time he fired the first shot until all the shooting was over?

A- I screamed and Jimmie turned around and said, "Shut up" and snapped this gun.

Q- You ducked behind the ironing board and raised up after that and you said that was when he was falling?

A- That is when he was falling.

Q- Where was he standing at that time?

A- Standing practically the same spot right at the trooper's head. He hadn't moved a muscle.

Q- He fell over on his left side?

A- Fell with his head toward the south.

Q- He didn't fall behind the door?

A- Yes, half of his body was behind the door. The door was half open. I can draw you a picture.

Q- What did you do then?

A- I just stood there and screamed for someone to come up. I think I screamed they were both dead. No one answered and no one came up. I thought the patrol was down at the door and thought they would come up. After they didn't come up I walked across, stepped over the patrol's body to step out of the door. I know his feet were kind of wedged between the screen and the facing of the door because I had to push hard to get it open. I just barely did get downstairs and they let me in the kitchen door.

Q- Do you know whether Nedimovich ever went out of the room from the time he walked over
   to the door?
A- I am positive he never stepped over the doorsill.

Q- He never went over the doorsill?
A- He never did.

Q- You watched him all the time except when you were behind the ironing board?
A- Dosing's body was right in the door. I am sure he never stepped over it. He stood practically in the same spot all the time.

Q- Now he hadn't gotten up and gone downstairs when you went down there?
A- No, it wasn't quite eleven when I went down.

Q- Were Mr. and Mrs. Coble downstairs when you went down there?
A- Yes, they were sitting down there reading the paper.

Q- Did Mr. Coble or Mrs. Coble say anything to you about the Packard car and Nedimovich?
A- No, they didn't. I think I said to Mrs. Coble, "I think we are going to Florida", something like that. She didn't have much to say, I noticed. I said, "Are you through with the paper? I want

to take it upstairs to read it." They said, "No." I said, "I will
get it later". I went upstairs and didn't have the slightest idea
there was anything.

Q- They didn't mention to you about the Little Rock business?
A- No.

Q- Was Mrs. Nix downstairs when you went down there?
A- Yes, she was, but she came up in just a few minutes.

Q- After you had gone back down there?
A- Yes.

Q- Did you ever touch any of the guns at all?
A- Yes, I touched one of them, but I had a handkerchief. When
I first went down there this Love, or whatever his name is,
was down there. He didn't think he was dead. I went down
screaming that they were both dead. So, the best I remember
he said, "You go up the road and tell those troopers they
are dead". I couldn't have walked up the road if I had had to.
There was a trooper out in the road. I don't know his name.
I went out there and told him they were both dead. He said
they might not be. We would better be careful. I said, "I will
go back up in front of you. You can come up behind me," and
we walked up. He gave me his handkerchief – I don't know
whether he is here or not. I don't think he is.

Q- Do you know who the patrol was that went up there?
A- No, I don't know. He was right behind me. I don't know who
he was. I had the crazy idea that if he wasn't dead and I could
get to their guns first, he wouldn't hurt anybody else. I picked
up the trooper's gun with the handkerchief and the patrol was

right behind me, and after they saw he was dead I put the gun down in the very same spot and went back downstairs.

Q- Were there any more shots fired after you saw him fall?
A- No, I am sure there wasn't.

Q- Everything was –
A- I was screaming and there wasn't any other sound.

Q- Did you ever see him point the gun at himself, his own head?
A- No, I didn't because I was behind the ironing board and just as I raised up he was falling and the gun was falling to the floor.

Q- What position was he in when you saw him fall?
A- When I saw him fall? He was standing practically facing the door.

Q- Do you know where the gun was?
A- No. It was falling to the floor when I turned around.

Q- Can you give us any idea how long you were ducked down behind the ironing board?
A- It was just a matter of seconds. I couldn't tell. I just ducked and raised up and that was all there was to it.

MR. CARR:
    Q- Any juror any question?

BY JUROR:
    Q- How about the remark Mr. Love said you made about he shot him?

A- He said, "Is he dead"? I said, "Yes, they are both dead". And then he said, "Did I shoot him"? I said, 'I don't know. He is dead is all I know."

BY MR. CARR:

Q- Did you ever say anything to John Love about having shot him?

A- Love having shot him?

Q- Yes.

A- No. He said, "Is he dead"? I said, "Yes, they are both dead", and he said, "I hope I shot him because he deserved it".

Q- That was after you got in the kitchen?

A- Yes. They thought I was scared, I guess I was taking on. He said, "Shut up. There is nothing wrong with you".

BY JUROR:

Q- You didn't say to Mr. Love, 'You shot him when he run up the steps"?

A- No.

BY MR. CARR:

Q- Did you ever say, "You shot him in both legs"?

A- No.

Q- Did you state to anybody that he was shot in both legs?

A- I think I said he is shot in his legs, but I believe that was because he fell over the trooper's body because his feet were lying right next to the trooper's head.

ANOTHER JUROR:

Q- How many shots did he shoot at the troopers?

A- The first one got Dosing. I don't know who the second hit, but it was fired down the stairway.

BY MR. CARR:

Q- Did this other trooper shoot him, or did you see?

A- No, I don't think the other trooper shot him.

Q- How many times do you say the big gun was shot?

A- I don't think Dosing ever shot it. I just believe it was shot once.

Q- That is when Jimmie had it?

A- Yes.

Q- Do you know whether Dosing had the gun out of the holster on his belt?

A- I kind of believe he did. I don't know for sure, but when he fell I think it fell out of his hand right at his head.

Q- Do you know – did you see Jimmie pick it up?

A- No, I didn't see Jimmie pick it up.

Q- You never did pick it up?

A- Yes, that trooper I told you, that patrolman that was with me when we came inside.

Q- Which one did you pick up, the big gun?

A- Yes, the big one. I had the crazy idea if I brought the gun downstairs there couldn't be any more shooting.

Q- Was the little gun still lying there?

A- Yes, I picked the big gun up and when I saw they were coming up there I laid it back down. I never did pick the little gun up.

Q- You stated the trooper gave you the handkerchief to put around it?

A- Yes, he did. It was a white handkerchief. I laid it on the ironing board. I don't know whether it is still there or not.

Q- You never have been on any trips with Nedimovich, have you, any out of town?

A- Yes, I went with him to take a girl friend down to Thayer, Missouri, once.

Q- When was that?

A- That was the first two weeks I knew him, when he called himself Donnahue. He had this Buick eight.

Q- That was back in September?

A- Yes, sir.

Q- This last month, had you been anywhere with him?

A- No. I had never been anywhere except around town since that trip.

Q- You had not been out of Springfield?

A- No. Yes, I did go to Halltown to my sister's, at Halltown.

BY THE CORONOR:

Q- You had never made any trips outside of Greene County?

A- Out of Greene County? No, I don't think so.

BY MR. CARR:

Q- Who was the girl you went to visit at Halltown?

A- She is my sister, Mrs. Cliffie Pringle.

Q- Who was it went to Thayer with you?

A- Velma Jones.

Q- Velma Jones?

A- Yes, she was from Thayer, Missouri, but she had been working at the Coffee Pot. She quit and wanted to go home so we took her.

Q- What did he say was his reason for changing his name?

A- He said when he came back – I didn't see him for almost a month – He told me his name was Nedimovich. Said he was going with a girl and told her his right name, and it was going to make a lot of trouble for him.

Q- Did he ever tell you where his home was?

A- Yes, Eveleth, Minnesota.

Q- He didn't say anything to you about this business down in Arkansas, did he?

A- No, he never said anything about having any trouble at all. When he came on this trip, I surely didn't know when he was coming, because he said he didn't know when he could come back because of the conditions at camp.

Q- Did he always seem to have plenty of money?

A- Sometimes he did and sometimes he didn't. He always said when he got paid was when he had money.

Q- You didn't know anything about him making that trade with the tire, did you, for gasoline?

A- No, I didn't.

Q- You didn't inquire whether he had enough money to go to Florida, did you?

A- Yes, I said, "What are we going to Florida on? Where are we going to get the money?" He said he had got out of the army and told me he was going to get a bonus next week.

Q- He was going on that bonus?

A- Yes, that is what he said.

Q- You didn't know how much money he was heaving town with?

A- No, I didn't.

Q- Has he been spending very much money the last few days? Did you notice the bills he had
been spending?

A- Not a lot. To tell the truth, I don't think I ever saw inside his pocketbook.

BY THE CORONER:

Q- Did you see any other gun in that room up there?

A- No, I didn't see any other gun.

Q- No other gun except these two guns in question?

A- Just those guns. That is the first gun I ever saw up there.

Q- You said a while ago you handled one of those guns. Could you shoot any?

A- No, I couldn't hit the side of a barn.

MR. Carr: That is all.

WITNESS EXCUSED

****

MR. EARL BARKLEY, being produced, sworn and examined, testified as follows:

EXAMINATION BY MR. CARR:

Q- State your name?

A- Earl Barkley.

Q- You are a member of the Highway Patrol of Missouri?

A- Yes, sir.

Q- Were you present at the Coffee Pot southeast, out south of Galloway yesterday around
noon?

A- Yes.

Q- What time did you go there, Mr. Barkley?

A- About twelve thirty, would be about my guess.

Q- Who did you go out with?

A- Sergeant Wallis, Trooper Bidewell and Trooper Grill the four of us.

Q- Had you received orders to go out there?

A- No. We had been to Dixon and were going home. We work out of Willow Springs. We left the office and were near the

National Cemetery when we got a radio call that this shooting had occurred, to go to the scene of the accident.

Q- You went right straight down there from the National Cemetery?

A- Yes, sir.

Q- What did you do when you got there?

A- The first car we saw was Graham's car. He was sitting in his car and it was sitting on the pavement just about two hundred and fifty feet this side of the station, and when he saw us he got out all bent over and said he had been shot. He told up this fellow was still upstairs. So Trooper Bidewell and I – I took the north side, Bidewell the south side, Trooper Grill stayed on the west, I believe, or the north side, and Sergeant Wallis west to the south side, and he looked around and talked to another fellow, talked to this girl, and looked around and said he was going upstairs, this back stairway.

Q- Wallis was the first man upstairs?

A- Yes.

Q- After the shooting?

A- Yes, sir.

Q- Did you to upstairs?

A- Yes, I did.

Q- You went up behind Wallis?

A- Yes.

Q- What did you find up there?

A- I walked up to the door and there lay Vic Dosing on his face, just inside the door, with his feet just across the doorsill, and the other boy, Nedimovich was kind of laying at right angle ith Trooper Dosing, and his head was kind of up against the wall and he was laying on his left side, with his arm kind of doubled back under him. His feet was right by Dosing's head.

Q- Where was Dosing struck, do you know?

A- I believe he was struck right in here, beside the nose and eye.

Q- Do you know where Nedimovich was struck?

A- Yes, he was struck on the right side of his head, and there was a large hole on this side. This hole had a strip of brains probably three inches long hanging out the hole.

Q- They were both dead when you got up there?

A- Yes, both dead.

Q- Did you find any gun up there?

A- Yes, two guns laying on the floor.

Q- What position?

A- Vic Dosing's gun was laying about two feet from Dosing's head, that is out in front of him, that would be to the east, and this other gun was laying just about a foot from Dosing's gun. Dosing's gun was a thirty- eight, special, Colt's thirty-eight special, and the other, the little gun was a thirty- eight Ivor Johnson, just an old owl head gun.

Q- A cheap gun?

A- Cheap gun, yes.

Q- Did you examine the guns to find how many shots had been fired?

A- Yes, I did.

Q- What did you find?

A- I believe the sheriff is the one that opened the guns and this owl gun had been fired twice and Vic's gun had been fired once.

Q- Four full cartridges?

A- Yes.

Q- This Owl gun had how many chambers?

A- I believe five.

Q- Two had been fired?

A- Two shots fired, yes. Two empty shells.

Q- Did you examine the place where the bullet went, the smaller hole on the right side of Nedimovich's head?

A- Yes, sir.

Q- Did you see any evidence of powder there?

A- Well, I don't believe I made quite that close an examination.

Q- Was there a smaller hole on th right side?

A- Yes, just a real little small hole on the right side, just about as large as your finger, just about the size of your finger, and on this side (left) a hole torn out as big as an egg, large as an egg.

Q- What else did you do while upstairs?

A- Just examined the whole building in general upstairs after the bodies were removed. We examined the men and the guns and after the bodies were removed we brought the girl upstairs and talked to her.

Q- You found no other gun upstairs?
A- No sir, no other gun.

Q- Did you find any evidence of where bullet slugs had struck around the door in the casing?
A- There was one bullet hole that had come right through a little glass pane, might have been a twenty inch pane in the door and there was one bullet hole through this glass pane in the door.

Q- Did you have any means of telling which way that bullet had gone through?
A- I don't believe I could say which way the bullet had went through.

Q- Where else did you find slug marks?
A- We found one place where apparently this bullet had come through between the outside back door, the side of the building and a place on the door handle, on the door just about the lock where the bullet had hit the door and glanced off, had not penetrated over about a quarter of an inch, and another bullet, a hole rather in the side of the door. It is kind of cardboard substance where it went through by the side of the door, and one in the ceiling, straight up in the ceiling.

Q- Can you place that one in the ceiling a little more particularly? What was it on a line with from the outside?

A- It wouldn't have been on a line from the outside. It would have been on a line from the inside.

Q- Where in the ceiling was the mark?

A- Like this was the door here, coming in from the stairway. It would be out just about as far as this from the door, and right straight up in the ceiling.

Q- A little past the center of the room?

A- Not quite the center.

Q- Were there any further bullet marks?

A- I believe that is all I observed.

Q- Just three?

A- Yes, that is all I observed. That is counting one bullet made two marks, where it came through the building and hit the door.

Q- Did you find any other marks of bullets downstairs?

A- Yes. We found – There is a little kitchen on the back of this Coffee Pot that is out square and right up in the corner there is a window facing the west and a window facing the south. There was a bullet hole in the south window, that would be the south window and aiso the west window had been fired from the inside, fired outside.

Q- The screen was bent out?

A- Yes, the screen was bent out.

BY JUROR:

    Q- That bullet in the building, that would have had to be shot from somewhere in the room?

    A- Yes.

    Q- That bullet could not have been fired by anyone outside?

    A- I don't believe it could. I think it had to be in the room.

    Q- It went through the room?

    A- Went right on through.

    Q- How big a hole where it went through the room?

    A- Just a real small one. This was the rear door.

    Q- What kind of room?

    A- Cardboard ceiling.

    Q- Paper cardboard?

    A- Paper cardboard that is what it was.

    Q- Couldn't that have been shot some other time?

    A- It looked like it was new. I examined it and it looked like it was fresh shot; no dust on it, just new.

    Q- Were there any shells shot out of Graham's gun?

    A- Graham brought his gun into the hospital with him, as far as I know. I don't know about that.

    Q- Just one shell shot out of Dosing's gun?

    A- Yes, just one shell out of Dosing's gun and two out of the other gun.

    Q- That is three bullets accounted for?

A- Yes.

ANOTHER JUROR:

Q- Those two downstairs were shot through the window?

A- Yes.

THE CORONER:

Q- That bullet hole you were talking about up in the ceiling, isn't it possible someone shot from down there, through that window and hit up there?

A- I don't think so.

JUROR:

Q- You said the hole, the bullet through the window couldn't have hit there?

A- Yes.

WITNESS EXCUSED

****

MR. RUEL WOMMACK, being produced, sworn and examined, testified as follows:

EXAMINATION BY MR. CARR:

Q- Sheriff, did you make an investigation of the shooting out at the Coffee Pot yesterday?

A- Yes, about twelve forty, when I got out there.

Q- Did you examine all the guns that were used out there?

A- Yes, sir.

Q- Do you know how many shots had been fired out of Vic Dosing's gun?

A- One.

Q- Did you examine the gun that Nedimovich used?

A- Yes.

Q- How many were fired from that?

A- Two.

Q- Was it a gun that had five chambers in it?

A- Yes.

Q- Three unused bullets in there?

A- Yes.

Q- Did you examine the gun of Trooper Graham?

A- No, sir.

Q- Do you know where that gun is?

A- No, sir.

Q- Did you examine the gun that was used by Mr. Stubbs?

A- No, sir.

Q- Or the gun used by Mr. Love?

A- No, sir.

Q- Do you know if any examination was made of those guns?

A- No, I don't personally know that. The only guns I examined were the two that were laying on the floor.

Q- You arrived out there at approximately the same time Mr. Wallis did, and Mr. Barkley?

A- When I arrived Trooper Barkley was at the head of the stair and Sergeant Wallis and some of the troopers were on the inside and Judge Stubbs was just outside.

Q- Did you find the bodies there in the same positions Trooper Barkley related?

A- Just exactly like Mr. Barkley described.

Q- Have you made an examination of the wound in the head of Nedimovich?

A- Yes, sir.

Q- State where the bullet entered his head.

A- Just over his right ear.

Q- Did it range upward or downward?

A- It seemed to have ranged upward and came out sort of the top part of his head.

Q- Did you examine the portion of skin or scalp around this place where the bullet entered?

A- Yes.

Q- What did you find there?

A- Powder marks.

Q- Were they distinct powder marks?

A- Yes.

Q- There is no doubt in your mind they were powder marks?

A- No, sir. It looked as though the gun had been held up to the head.

Q- Was there a distinct ring around the small wound?
A- Yes, a distinct ring.

Q- You examined that yesterday?
A- Last night, yes.

Q- You examined it again today?
A- Yes.

Q- Was it more visible last night than it is today, the ring?
A- Yes, sir.

BY JUROR:

Q- Ruel, that bullet now – You say he killed himself. Could that have been the bullet that went through his head and went up in the ceiling, taking that angle, him being in this door, could that go on up in the ceiling?
A- I don't remember seeing the hole in the ceiling myself. I know I saw one in the cardboard. I saw that and the one in the window pane, but I don't remember seeing the one in the ceiling.

Q- Possibly turned, the way that hole looked in his head it cold have gone up in the ceiling because it was going upward?
A- It should be bent this angle.

Q- From where I was standing I thought possibly that could be the one that went up in the ceiling?
A- Possibly could, but I didn't see that hole.

ANOTHER JUROR:

Q- If the gun was away from the man's head there wouldn't have been no powder burns?

A- If it had been twenty-four inches or over it would have been splattered.

Q- Not as compact as it was?

A- No, it would have been more scattered. I might tell you one thing. That gun, that little gun was cocked at the time I picked it up and examined it and evidently was jammed, because last night we tried the gun out, shot a couple of shots out of it, and in the second shot it jammed.

Q- Is that the little thirty-eight?

A- The little thirty-eight.

Q- That is the gun that killed Vic Dosing?

A- It was cocked at the time I picked it up and evidently jammed. I didn't pull the trigger. I was scared to pull the trigger. Sergeant Viets tried it and it did jam.

Q- Was it loaded?

A- It had two empties and three unfired shells.

Q- The other shell was in the chamber, was it, the barrel?

A- Yes, three shells were in the cylinder and two had been fired out.

Q- A while ago they mentioned something about an owl head gun. Is that the gun, you have reference to?

A- Yes, that is it. The trooper made a mistake. It is a Herrington and Richardson instead of an Ivor Johnson.

Q- You didn't see the bullet that went through his head? You didn't see where it went out?

A- I have not been back down there, but it seems to me I saw a mark in the wall there on the south side. I don't think it went through there. I just can't remember definitely. There was quite a lot of excitement there trying to get the bodies out, to see what we could find, etc. I can't remember that, but it seems to me like I saw marks of a gun on that side.

Q- That wouldn't be on the line with Stubb's firing?

A- No, that would be in the line probably –

Q- Of where he stood?

A- Yes, that is the best I remember.

WITNESS EXCUSED

****

SERGEANT O. L. VIETS, being produced, sworn and examined, testified as follows:

EXAMINATION BY MR. CARR:

Q- Sergeant Viets, will you please tell the jury what investigation you made of the bullet marks

in the building upstairs in the Coffee Pot?

A- Well, I made practically the same investigation that Mr. Barkley testified, or the sheriff. I came out to the place right after these other patrol had got out there, and I believe I walked up with one of them upstairs and my investigation there would be the same as his testimony with the exception I might add to it that we went back there last night and probed in some of the holes for the bullets Trooper Barkley mentioned. For instance, the bullet that come probably from the door of the place and went up through the ceiling, that is panel board. We took that down and could spot the bullet as it went through the roof. It went clear on through the roof. It would be in line almost with the hole in the glass or it could possibly have been the bullet that killed the soldier. If he were standing, the bullet that killed him entered about his right ear and came out here (indicting). That could be the bullet that went through the roof. It could be the bullet.

BY THE CORONER:

Q- Is it possible that hole up there is in line with the hole in the door?

A- The ceiling is here and roof top above, and that goes on an angle where it entered the roof, where it went through the ceiling. That would indicate it went on an angle. It could have come through the stairway and the door up there, or could be the bullet that went through the soldier's head.

Q- It ranged upward from the place where the bullet entered his head. Where it came out, is that sufficient to place it in line with the hole?

A- Yes.

Q- Of the man standing up?

A- Yes, we tried to check it, three or four of us, and gauging from the angle it came out, a man six feet in height standing next to the door, would put the bullet practically where it entered the ceiling and came out through the roof. Or if a man was standing in the door of the stair, the range through the glass would be practically the same that goes through the roof.

Q- Did you examine the scalp and skin of Nedimovich for powder burns?

A- I did last night.

Q- Did you find some?

A- Yes.

Q- Powder around the wound?

A- Definite powder burns around the wound. The wound where it entered the small hole, where the bullet hit, around that I would say the size of a finger, where the skin is torn out and definitely black where the powder burned, and on this side (indicating), where the bullet came out, it pushed out. And there was a wound there, oh, this long (indicating) where it seems the skull cracked and pushed out and apparently pushed some of the brains out through there which was also on the floor in a pool of blood. And that would indicate that the bullet had been right at his head, because the concussion of the force of that caused this to bulge out behind (indicating). If it had been any distance, it would not have had a tendency to bulge out.

Q- You have seen similar wounds where you knew the gun was fired at close range?

A- Yes. I think there is one other bullet that there might be some doubt about, and that is the bullet that lodged in the door next to the door handle, when that door is opened and fired from the outside, like a bullet had entered from the outside, came through the outside wall. Then there is a space, say about six inches in there. We probed through that with a wire that pointed directly the bullet marks in the door, and that bullet had penetrated through a quarter of an inch and dropped down. I think the sheriff has that bullet.

Q- What line did that wire point?

A- From the outside, the hole in the door, the hole where the bullet had struck and fell down.

Q- Could you tell approximately from where that bullet had been fired?

A- The stairway runs down in this direction and it is on the top toward the west and south here, and this bullet had been fired from the south of the stairway or south of the building in that direction.

BY JUROR:

Q- Probably a lighter type of gun than the regular officer's thirty-eight?

A- I don't know about that. The bullet has been examined. I had in mind it was a thirty-eight.

ANOTHER JUROR:

Q- That bullet that went through that ceiling – that would have to be a pretty good gun to go all the way through?

A- Yes, it would take a high powered gun. I don't believe the soldier's gun would have given that much penetration.

Q- The trooper's gun would, Dosing's?

A- Yes, the trooper's gun or the gun the justice of the peace was firing.

BY MR. CARR:

Q- This is a thirty-eight?

A- Yes, that is a thirty-eight. That fits in the mark in the door. It went in sideways and made an impression of about half the diameter of the bullet and then fell to the floor, and that bullet came from the outside.

Q- That is Vic's gun, the big one?

A- Yes, that fired the same type of bullet and I expect the gun of Judge Stubbs would have the same shell.

Q- Do you know how many times Judge Stubbs fired?

A- He shot once. I didn't examine his gun, but I talked to him this morning. Others had examined it and he told me this morning he shot once. Dosing's gun had been shot once and this gun (the smaller one) had been fired twice.

Q- Mr. Graham never did get in the room, did he?

A- No, what he told me, he was three or four steps down.

Q- That shot he fired could have gone in that ceiling at that angle?

A- Possibly. He told me this morning he didn't have any chance to fire until after Vic fell because the stairway is narrow. He was directly behind him.

BY JUROR:

Q- Was the other patrol in uniform – Barkley, is that his name?

A- Yes, they were all in uniform.

BY THE CORONER:

Q- I inquired a little while ago, if you found any other shells. (Producing long shell).

A- It was in the dresser drawer. The bullet was in that pouch and was in the dresser drawer in the room. Some ammunition they used in the army probably.

BY MR. CARR:

Q- Did you make any examination of his physical effects?

A- Well, the sheriff had arrived about that time and I got a call to report in the office when through. I asked the sheriff if he would take charge of all personal effects of the soldier, everything he could find, and keep it in his custody.

WITNESS EXCUSED

****

BY MR. CARR: Judge, you might state to the jury where you found this paper (birth certificate).

THE CORONER: I think we found that in his billfold. Didn't we, Sheriff? In his billfold.

MR. U. R. COBLE, being produced, sworn and examined, testified as follows:

EXAMINATION BY MR. CARR:

Q- State your name, please?

A- U. R. Coble

Q- You own and operate the Coffee Pot?

A- Yes.

Q- Do you know when Milan Nedimovich arrived in Springfield Saturday night?

A- The first I seen of him was somewhere around ten thirty, and I can't recall –

Q- He came in the downstairs part?
A- Yes.

Q- Do you know what kind of car he was in?
A- I didn't right at the time, but I stepped outside. We were busy when he first came up, and he didn't come up when he first drove in the Coffee Pot. He stayed on the outside. When I got a slack period I stepped to the back door and I saw it was a Packard coupe.

Q- Did you get such an idea before the shooting occurred?
A- Sunday morning.

Q- What was it gave you that impression?
A- I saw an article in the Sunday morning paper.

Q- The fact that it was a Packard coupe?
A- Yes, describing this killing in Arkansas and there had been a Packard coupe stolen and this coupe he was driving answered that description.

Q- Did you talk about that to your wife?
A- Yes, I showed her the article in the paper.

Q- What time was that?
A- Must have been somewhere around ten thirty, a quarter to eleven, something like that.

Q- When, was it Margie came downstairs that morning?

A- It was just as she came down there because I had not seen the article in the paper when she came down. Just after that. I was reading the paper at the time she was down there I had started in. The article was over in the paper two or three sheets. I was turning through, glancing through the paper and happened to notice this article and read it.

Q- She ate her breakfast and went back upstairs, did she?
A- Yes, sir.

Q- Where was Mrs. Nix?
A- She was downstairs when Margie was down there and she stayed downstairs.

Q- She didn't go back upstairs?
A- No.

Q- You knew he was upstairs Sunday morning?
A- I did when they came down for breakfast.

Q- But you didn't know he had come in early that morning?
A- I didn't.

Q- Did Margie ever come back downstairs again before noon?
A- I don't think she did.

Q- You or your wife, so far as you know, never said anything to her about this article you read
 in the paper?
A- No, we never said anything to her.

Q- Where were you when the troopers drove up there?

A- Inside the Coffee Pot when they drove up, out in front. I met them at the door.

Q- The front door?
A- Yes, sir.

Q- Did they enter the Coffee Pot?
A- They entered the Coffee Pot.

Q- What did they say to you?
A- They wanted to know where this man was.

Q- Had there been somebody else inquiring about them?
A- Mr. Love.

Q- What had you told him?
A- He came up, drove up out in front and came inside and ordered a coke. I was getting it and he turned around and said, "Is that a Packard coupe outside"? and wanted to know if it belonged to me. He wanted to know if he was about and I told him he was upstairs. He said his car was parked there out south of the Coffee Pot, right in the driveway. And he drove up and turned around in the highway and went south. As to where he went, I don't know. And just in, oh, two or three minutes, probably that long, or longer, I noticed his car was back down south of the Coffee Pot on the east side of the road. I didn't know whether he was going to call the troopers or who was going to call them or whether he would go back up to Mr. Stubbs and wait until this boy would probably leave or something like that. And I judge it was fifteen minutes, probably twenty, when the state patrol car came up to the front door.

Q- They entered and came through the downstairs?

A- They entered the front door.

Q- What did they say to you?

A- They wanted to know where this fellow was at. I told them upstairs, and they wanted to know how to get up there. I told them to go out through the Coffee Pot, out the back door and there was a stairway leading up there. And Mr. Love was constable and he came in through the door about the same time they were going through the kitchen of the Coffee Pot, he come in through the front door.

Q- Where did the officers go?

A- They went out through the back door. I didn't follow them.

Q- All three of them?

A- Yes.

Q- Did you hear them going upstairs?

A- Yes.

Q- You didn't go out and look?

A- No.

Q- What did you do while they were going up steps?

A- My wife and two children and Lela Nix were on the inside and we were worried if any shooting would take place, worried about the children.

Q- Did the officers have any guns out?

A- They did not.

Q- Did you see them pull their guns out when going up the stairs?

A- No, I could hear them going up the steps and that is all.

Q- What happened after that?

A- The shooting taken place. There were some shots fired and Mr. Love came back in at the back door, and Mr. Graham also came in the back door, came through and wanted to know if we had a telephone, Trooper Graham, and I told him we didn't have. He said he was going to have to get help from somewhere, and about that time he jumped in his car. It was headed south. He just wheeled it around in the road and came back north.

Q- Did you know whether he was struck at that time?

A- I didn't know.

Q- Did you see Nedimovich come downstairs at any time?

A- When the trooper left. He came downstairs about the time the trooper was leaving, I think, I won't be positive about it. It all happened so quick. You can't remember all of it.

Q- You did see him on the stairway?

A- Yes, sir.

Q- How far did he come down?

A- Come down to the landing where it turns back north two more steps, where it turns to the kitchen. He came down to that landing and Mr. Love fired a shot out the window, the west window at him and he turned around, the soldier boy did, and started up the steps, and he fired another shot out the south window.

Q- At that time Graham had gone out the front?

A- Yes, out the front door. Just about that time was when he asked if we had a telephone.

Q- Did you hear any more shots after those two fired by Love?

A- I don't think. There could have been possibly a shot fired, but I don't know.

Q- Did Margie ever try to come down the steps?

A- She came down, oh, I judge approximately two or three minutes after that, she came down the steps.

Q- That is when she came in the kitchen?

A- She fell down at the back door.

Q- Did you hear any shots between the two shots fired by Love out the south window and the time Margie came down stairs?

A- No.

Q- You don't recall any?

A- No.

Q- From where Love shot out the south window he was in too low a position to have shot Nedimovich in the head?

A- He would shoot him in the legs. He was standing down on a level with the window.

Q- Did you see Mr. Stubbs?

A- No, I didn't see Mr. Stubbs because we were on the inside. I didn't even know he was out there.

Q- You didn't hear any gun go off upstairs, did you, again after that?

A- Not that I know.

Q- How long was it between the time Nedimovich went back upstairs and Margie came down?

A- It was probably two or three minutes, more or less.

Q- Did she make any noise upstairs?

A- She was screaming.

Q- Who went upstairs beside – Who was the next person that went upstairs after Nedimovich came down and ran back upstairs?

A- I don't know because I didn't go outside.

Q- You were still in the main part downstairs?

A- I was still in the main room downstairs.

Q- Was your wife in there with you?

A- She was in there.

Q- She was not back in the kitchen?

A- No.

Q- Was Mrs. Nix in there all the time with you?

A- Yes, she was in there.

Q- Where you couldn't see what was going on outside?

A- No.

Q- Other than what took place in the kitchen?

A- Not after he ran downstairs and ran back up.

Q- All you saw there was out the kitchen window, is that right?
A- Yes, sir.

Q- You and your wife and Mrs. Nix, or anybody that you know of
had any talk with Margie
about this Little Rock suspicion at all?
A- No.

BY JUROR:

Q- If that gun had been shot after Margie came down, you could
have heard it, couldn't you?
A- We probably could, but we were worried. The state trooper
pulling out left nobody there but us and Mr. Love here and his
gun was jammed at that time. There was no other gun we had
down there. I didn't have any gun at all.

Q- You heard Margie testify he didn't come down the steps?
A- Yes, I heard that.

Q- And you say he did come down the steps?
A- Yes.

BY THE CORONER:

Q- Did he have a gun in his hand?
A- I couldn't see; I could just see his legs.

BY MR. CARR:

Q- Did you know him any length of time?

A- I have known him since the latter part of September. I got acquainted with him through him coming down there to see Margie.

Q- Had you made any trips with him at any time?
A- No trips.

BY THE CORONER:

Q- That hole in the door, do you have any idea whether it was shot from the outside or the inside?
A- The door upstairs?

Q- Yes.
A- No, I don't have any idea.

WITNESS EXCUSED

****

MRS. LELA NIX, being produced, sworn and examined, testified as follows:

EXAMINATION BY MR. CARR:

Q- Your name is Mr. Lela Nix?
A- Yes.

Q- Where do you live?
A- At Galloway.

Q- Did you spend Saturday night at the Coffee Pot?
A- Yes, sir.

Q- You stayed upstairs and slept upstairs that night?

A- Yes, sir.

Q- Who else was there that night?
A- Well, I was there upstairs, there. Margie and Jimmie come in, I don't know what time it was. I didn't look at my watch. She said it was between three and four.

Q- Did you wake up when they came home?
A- Yes, I unlocked the door and let them in.

Q- That door is locked by means of a drop?
A- Yes.

Q- Was Jimmie or Nedimovich with her when she came home?
A- Yes, sir.

Q- He came upstairs with her?
A- Yes. She came up first and she said, "Lela, will it be all right for Jimmie to stay up here until morning"?

Q- (Addressing the jury) Did you hear that?
A- She came up a little before he did and said, "Lela, will it be all right for jimmie to stay up here until morning"? I said, "Margie" – I was sleepy and I said, "Suit yourself". So he stayed.

Q- Where did she put him?
A- He slept on the studio couch.

Q- That was over on the north side of the room?
A- Yes.

Q- The bed you and Margie usually sleep on, on Saturday nights was over in the south side of the room?

A- Yes.

Q- What time did you get up the next morning?

A- Between nine and nine thirty, sometime around there.

Q- Neither one of them had got up yet?

A- Yes.

Q- Did you go downstairs?

A- After I dressed I went down.

Q- When did you next see Margie?

A- When she came down for breakfast.

Q- What time was that?

A- That wasn't long after I went down.

Q- An hour or so?

A- Around an hour, I guess.

Q- Did she go back upstairs as soon as she had eaten?

A- Yes, sir.

Q- Did Nedimovich ever come down?

A- No.

Q- Did you go back upstairs?

A- Yes, I went up two or three times.

Q- Two or three times?

A- Yes, sir. I didn't stay long. I would come down, see. I was just up and down.

Q- She was up there all morning, except the time she came down and ate her breakfast?

A- Yes.

Q- Is that correct?

A- Yes.

Q- Do you know when he got up?

A- No, he wasn't up when I was up there the last time.

Q- He wasn't up then?

A- No.

Q- What time was that?

A- Well, I guess it was between ten thirty and eleven, the last time I came downstairs.

Q- Did you have any conversation with the Cobles about this Little Rock matter?

A- Margie, when she was down there, was talking about going to her sister's that afternoon, but she was going to help us out in the afternoon through the busy time if Mrs. Coble wanted her to. And Mrs. Coble told her to go ahead and take off because she probably wouldn't need her. She went on upstairs and she said that Mrs. Coble said it would be all right for her to go on to her sister's.

BY JUROR:

Q- How may rooms have you upstairs?

A- One large room.

BY MR. CARR:

    Q- The question I asked you – Do you know whether Mr. and Mrs. Coble said anything to her about the Little Rock matter?

    A- No, they did not.

    Q- Did they say anything to you?

    A- He came over after she went upstairs and showed me the paper, what he had seen in the paper.

    Q- Was she ever back downstairs?

    A- No. But we talked about it. I told him to go out and get the license number and he did, and we were talking about what we ought to do, and it was just about five or ten minutes before this Mr. love came in.

    Q- Where were you when the patrol car drove in front?

    A- I was standing in the kitchen.

    Q- The kitchen is in the back part?

    A- Yes, sir.

    Q- Did you say there in the kitchen when they came in?

    A- Yes, sir.

    Q- Did you see them go on upstairs?

    A- Yes, sir.

    Q- What else did you see?

A- That is all I seen. I seen them go around the corner and I left out of the kitchen there and went in behind the counter. Mr. Love got in front of this kitchen window.

Q- He got in front of the kitchen window?

A- Yes, and was looking out the south window.

Q- He went upstairs with Graham and Dosing, didn't he?

A- I don't know whether he did nor not.

Q- You don't know?

A- I believe he went out the back door, but I wouldn't swear whether he did or not, because, you know, I didn't look all the time. I was in the kitchen and out in front.

Q- You didn't see Mr. Graham and Dosing go up the steps?

A- No.

Q- Where were you when you heard the first shot?

A- I don't remember. I guess I was in behind the counter or in the kitchen. I wouldn't say because I don't remember.

Q- You were not where you could see the stairway?

A- Well, part of the time I was.

Q- Did you see anybody on the stairway?

A- Yes, I seen somebody on the stairway, but I couldn't tell who it was.

Q- You couldn't tell whether it was the patrol or who it was?

A- No.

Q- Do you have any idea how the shots were fired, whether there were two right together, or what do you know?

A- All I know, they seemed to be popping around petty fast.

Q- You don't remember whether there were two right there at the first, or how they happened?

A- I know that Mr. Love shot out the window in the kitchen.

Q- He shot twice?

A- Yes, sir.

Q- One out of each window?

A- I guess he did. I think he is the one that shot the two panes of the windows in the kitchen.

Q- You never did go out of the kitchen until all of the shooting was over, did you?

A- No.

Q- Did you ever see Nedimovich on the stairway?

A- No. I don't know about that. I told you I didn't know who it was went up and down the stairway.

Q- You know Graham and Dosing went up?

A- I seen them going out the back door. I think Mr. Love went out there, but I don't know how far he got up the stairs or anything about it.

Q- Did you see anybody on the stairway after that, through the windows, or anywhere else?

A- Well, no, I don't think so. Just the one time when, they were doing all this shooting.

Q- Who was that you saw?

A- I don't know. I couldn't tell who it was, but I guess it was Mr. Graham.

Q- Did you see anything of a gun up there?

A- No, sir.

Q- That morning in your two or three trips back upstairs?

A- No, sir.

Q- Did you see anything out of the way going on when you would be back upstairs?

A- No.

Q- How long was it between the time Love came and asked for him until the patrol car drove in?

A- I guess about ten or fifteen minutes.

Q- About ten or fifteen minutes?

A- I guess, I don't know. It couldn't have been very long.

Q- You didn't go up there during that time, did you?

A- No.

BY JUROR:

Q- Did the soldier have a grip with him that night, a suit case, or just come up there?

A- When he came up in the morning?

Q- That night, at three o'clock in the morning. Do you know whether he had a suitcase with him or not?

A- No, he didn't have any baggage.

Q- He didn't have any baggage of any kind?

A- No.

Q- Didn't even have any package or anything?

A- No, I didn't see anything.

ANOTHER JUROR:

Q- Had he stayed there all night that you know of at any other time than last Saturday?

A- That is all I know of. The first time I ever seen the boy was a week Saturday night; the first time I ever seen him.

BY THE CORONER:

Q- Did you see these guns up there in that room?

A- No, sir.

Q- Did you see any other gun around?

A- No, sir.

Q- At any time?

A- No, sir.

BY JUROR: Judge, how much money did he have with him?

THE CORONER: He didn't seem to have anything much. Sheriff, do you remember how much money we found?

SHERIFF: It is right in there. (The billford) Twenty cents, or something like that.

ANOTHER JUROR: (Of Mr. Coble)

Q- Had he stayed there at any other time at night that you know of?

A- Not that I know of. When he first began coming down there, he slept out in his car one night unbeknown to me.

Q- He could have run in there at that hour of night and you wouldn't know it?

A- Sometime ago he did.

WITNESS EXCUSED

****

THE CORONER: Any other witness:

MR. CARR: I believe that is all.

WHEREUPON, the jury, having been duly charged by the Acting Coroner to diligently find, and true presentment make, as to the manner in which the deceased, Victor Dosing and Milan Nedimovich, came to their deaths, and having been given two forms for verdicts, retired to the jury room to consider the testimony and the facts presented, and returned the following verdicts:

STATE OF MISSOURI

County of Greene,

We, the jury, having been duly sworn and affirmed by G. H. Boehm, Acting Coroner of Greene County, Missouri, diligently to find and true presentment make in what manner and by whom VICTOR DOSING, whose dead body was found at the Herman Lohmeyer Funeral Home, on the 8th day of December, 1941, came to his death, after having heard the evidence and upon full inquiry concerning the facts and a careful examination of said body, do find that the deceased came to his death as follows:

We, the jury, have come to a decision that Vic Dosing came to his death by a gunshot fired from the hands of Milan Nedimovich by using a .38 Herrington Richardson revolver.

(Signed)
Miles J. Walker, Foreman
W. F. Wieck
Tom Fielder
Roy J Chaffin
Charles D. Martin
G. L. Alsup

STATE OF MISSOURI
County of Greene

We, the jury, having been duly sworn and affirmed by F. H. Boehm, Acting Coroner of Greene County, Missouri, diligently to find and true presentment make in what manner and by whom MILAN NEDIMOVICH whose dead body was found at the Herman Lohmeyer Funeral Home, on the 8th day of December, 1941, came to his death, after having heard the evidence and upon full inquiry concerning the facts and a careful examination of said body, do find that the deceased came to his death as follows: We the jury, find that the said Milan Nedimovich came to his death by his own hand, self-inflicted, using Vic Dosing's 38 Police Special.

(Signed)
Miles N. Walker, foreman
W. F. Wieck
Tom Fielder

Roy J. Chaffin

Charles D. Martin

G. L. Alsup

STATE OF MISSOURI

County of Greene.

I, G. H. Boehm, Acting Coroner, Greene County, Missouri, certify that an inquest at the time and place mentioned, over the dead bodies of Victor Dosing and Milan Nedimovich, who were supposed to come to their deaths by violence, the following witnesses: John Love; F. A. Stubbs; Miss Margie Smith; Earl Barkley; Ruel Wommack; O.L. Viets; U. R. Coble; Mrs. Lela Nix, were sworn to testify the whole truth of their knowledge touching the matter in connection wherewith, were examined and their examinations were taken down in shorthand by Carrie L. Hopwood, reporter, and afterward typed by her, and testimony of the said witnesses, with the verdict of the jury, is now herewith returned.

Given under my hand, at Springfield, in said county and state, this 8th day of December, A.D. 1941.

_____ G. H. Boehm _____

Acting Coroner of Greene

County, Missouri